"You're doing *what?*"

Dylan stared at Julie and tried to comprehend what she'd just said.

"You heard me. I'm putting a stop to all of this." Her gaze rose from the child resting in her arms. "I can't do it anymore."

"You can't do what? Stay alive? Stay safe?"

"Safe?" She shook her head. "Like Hattie? Lord, she was miles from civilization and he still found her. He'll find me, too. He'll find *us*." She stared down at the small boy in her arms and touched his chubby cheek. "I won't run anymore, Dylan," she said, a tear sliding from the corner of her eye.

"Are you crazy?" he demanded. "You can't just sit here and wait for those guys to catch up."

"I'm not going to."

Dylan's feeling of relief was short-lived when he heard her next words. "I'm going after him."

Dear Reader,

Being born and bred in the Lone Star state, I was particularly thrilled when Harlequin invited me to write a story for the TRUEBLOOD, TEXAS continuity series.

Dylan's Destiny features Dylan Garrett, ex-cop turned private investigator, who is a Texan through and through. He's loyal and strong and determined to save the woman he loves from a power-hungry mob boss eager to silence her for good.

Love?

While Julie Cooper appreciates Dylan's help—they've been the best of friends since college—she's hesitant to believe he's motivated by such a fierce emotion.

But as danger closes in and Julie finds herself on the run for her very life, she soon realizes that this Texan's love is Trueblood true. Dylan turns out to be more than Julie's friend and protector. He's her destiny, and she's his.

I hope you enjoy reading *Dylan's Destiny*. I love to hear from readers—you can write to me c/o Harlequin Enterprises, 225 Duncan Mill Road, Don Mills, Ontario M3B 3K9, Canada.

Take care, and happy reading from deep in the heart!

Kimberly Raye

TRUEBLOOD, TEXAS

Kimberly Raye

Dylan's Destiny

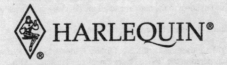

HARLEQUIN®

TORONTO • NEW YORK • LONDON
AMSTERDAM • PARIS • SYDNEY • HAMBURG
STOCKHOLM • ATHENS • TOKYO • MILAN • MADRID
PRAGUE • WARSAW • BUDAPEST • AUCKLAND

Kimberly Raye is acknowledged
as the author of this work.

For Curt,
For being my very own Trueblood, Texas hero.
I love you, baby!

HARLEQUIN BOOKS
225 Duncan Mill Road, Don Mills,
Ontario, Canada M3B 3K9

ISBN 0-373-65089-2

DYLAN'S DESTINY

Copyright © 2001 by Harlequin Books S.A.

Visit us at www.eHarlequin.com

Printed in U.S.A.

TRUEBLOOD, TEXAS

THE TRUEBLOOD LEGACY

THE YEAR WAS 1918, and the Great War in Europe still raged, but Esau Porter was heading home to Texas.

The young sergeant arrived at his parents' ranch northwest of San Antonio on a Sunday night, only the celebration didn't go off as planned. Most of the townsfolk of Carmelita had come out to welcome Esau home, but when they saw the sorry condition of the boy, they gave their respects quickly and left.

The fever got so bad so fast that Mrs. Porter hardly knew what to do. By Monday night, before the doctor from San Antonio made it into town, Esau was dead.

The Porter family grieved. How could their son have survived the German peril, only to burn up and die in his own bed? It wasn't much of a surprise when Mrs. Porter took to her bed on Wednesday. But it was a hell of a shock when half the residents of Carmelita came down with the horrible illness. House after house was hit by death, and all the townspeople could do was pray for salvation.

None came. By the end of the year, over one hundred souls had perished. The influenza virus took those in the prime of life, leaving behind an unprecedented number of orphans. And the virus knew no boundaries. By the time the threat had passed, more than thirty-seven million people had succumbed worldwide.

But in one house, there was still hope.

Isabella Trueblood had come to Carmelita in the late 1800s with her father, blacksmith Saul Trueblood, and her mother, Teresa Collier Trueblood. The family had traveled from Indiana, leaving their Quaker roots behind.

Young Isabella grew up to be an intelligent woman who had a gift for healing and storytelling. Her dreams centered on the boy next door, Foster Carter, the son of Chester and Grace.

Just before the bad times came in 1918, Foster asked Isabella to be his wife, and the future of the Carter spread was secured. It was a happy union, and the future looked bright for the young couple.

Two years later, not one of their relatives was alive. How the young couple had survived was a miracle. And during the epidemic, Isabella and Foster had taken in more than twenty-two orphaned children from all over the county. They fed them, clothed them, taught them as if they were blood kin.

Then Isabella became pregnant, but there were complications. Love for her handsome son, Josiah, born in 1920, wasn't enough to stop her from growing weaker by the day. Knowing she couldn't leave her husband to tend to all the children if she died, she set out to find families for each one of her orphaned charges.

And so the Trueblood Foundation was born. Named in memory of Isabella's parents, it would become famous all over Texas. Some of the orphaned children went to strangers, but many were reunited with their families. After reading notices in newspapers and church bulletins, aunts, uncles, cousins and grandparents rushed to Carmelita to find the young ones they'd given up for dead.

Toward the end of Isabella's life, she'd brought together more than thirty families, and not just her orphans. Many others, old and young, made their way to her doorstep, and Isabella turned no one away.

At her death, the town's name was changed to Trueblood, in her honor. For years to come, her simple grave was adorned with flowers on the anniversary of her death, grateful tokens of appreciation from the families she had brought together.

Isabella's son, Josiah, grew into a fine rancher and married Rebecca Montgomery in 1938. They had a daughter, Elizabeth Trueblood Carter, in 1940. Elizabeth married her neighbor William Garrett in 1965, and gave birth to twins Lily and Dylan in 1971, and daughter Ashley a few years later. Home was the Double G ranch, about ten miles from Trueblood proper, and the Garrett children grew up listening to stories of their famous great-grandmother, Isabella. Because they were Truebloods, they knew that they, too, had a sacred duty to carry on the tradition passed down to them: finding lost souls and reuniting loved ones.

CHAPTER ONE

HE WAS TOO LATE.

The thought hammered through Dylan Garrett's head as he slammed his foot down on the gas pedal. The Jeep Wrangler sucked gas and roared down the dark stretch of Interstate 10, gobbling up pavement the way his prized black Lab, Dallas, ate up a convict's scent.

He couldn't be too late. He *wouldn't* be.

Dylan had spent the past ten years since he'd met Julie Matthews Cooper being too late. Time had beat him at every turn. He'd been too late to make an impression before his best friend won her heart. Too late to declare his feelings and beg her not to marry his friend. Too late to save her when that friend had turned from her husband into her enemy. Too late to help her through a difficult pregnancy spent alone and on the run.

No more.

The highway markers blurred past him as he

drove faster, leaving the bright lights of San Antonio and heading north toward Boot Hill. His heart pounded as he descended the exit ramp and headed through the quiet Texas town. Quiet, as in calm, undisturbed, *safe*.

That's why he'd picked it as an ideal hiding place for Julie Cooper. His old college buddy. His dearest friend. The love of his life.

If only she knew.

The Jeep roared louder as he checked his mirrors before zooming through a red light. He'd been standing up as best man at Max and Rachel Santana's wedding when he'd received Julie's frantic call. Rushing off before the ceremony had barely begun, Dylan had foregone any timely apologies. If anyone would understand his quick disappearance, it was Max and Rachel. Their road to happiness had been rocky at best, after Max learned that Rachel had given up her baby daughter for adoption. Now that the three of them were reunited, their future looked bright indeed.

Things were different for Dylan and Julie. There would be no happily ever after. No two-story house with a sprawling oak tree out front. No wraparound porch littered with toys and kids.

Forget day-to-day living with its ups and downs. Tears and laughter. Joys and sorrow. The future centered around survival, which was why Dylan had hauled ass out of the reception, much to his family's dismay.

But Boot Hill was a long drive from Trueblood, Texas, and Dylan prayed he would make it in time.

By late afternoon he swerved into the small apartment complex just off Main Street. Another turn around one of the corner buildings and he caught sight of her second-story apartment. Fear slithered around his spine and squeezed tight as his gaze snagged on the large front window.

The drapes sat open, revealing the living room where he'd sat on the sofa as often as he could during the past few months and shared Julie's favorite pineapple-and-jalapeno pizza.

Not tonight.

There'd be no Victorian lamp burning on the end table. No vanilla-scented potpourri candle casting lively shadows against the peach-colored walls. No television set blasting the latest San Antonio Spurs game. Tonight they would be on the run.

The whole building seemed deserted. Empty. Dead.

His gut twisted at the thought, the feeling all too familiar after years of undercover work with the Dallas Police Department. He'd traded police work for private investigation a couple of years back, but his instincts hadn't faded. In fact, they'd sharpened and become even more reliable. It was a characteristic that made him good at his job. The best when it came to reading people and situations.

Too late.

His skin prickled and his stomach churned as he shoved the Jeep into park, killed the engine and jumped out. He hit the stairs two at a time, panic pushing him faster.

He thought of the small child Julie had given birth to only eight short months ago—little Thomas with his silky black hair and chubby cheeks—and his heart pounded even faster.

They had to be okay. They *had* to.

Cold metal met warm flesh as his fingers closed around the doorknob. He paused, his heart pounding, fear gripping every nerve.

"Please." He whispered the same prayer he'd prayed time and time again during the year he'd spent searching for Julie after her sudden disappearance. When the leads became too few and the future looked grim. When he'd been so close to giving up and admitting the worst to himself.

But he hadn't. He'd ignored his fear and finally he'd found her.

Now he might have lost her again.

"No," he growled as he tried the door.

The knob turned, but the door wouldn't budge. Several things registered in that next charged instant. The dead bolt was in place, which meant the door was locked from the inside.

Before he could stop to think what he was doing, Dylan pulled his fist back then smashed it into the window.

He'd given her up once without a fight and it wasn't going to happen again. Julie Cooper was his responsibility, his life, his heart, even if she didn't know it.

Till death do us part.

That's how long his love would last for Julie.

If only he didn't have the sick, gut-wrenching feeling that that moment had finally come.

SHE WAS DEAD.

Julie fought for a frantic breath and tried to control the hammering of her heart. She refused to accept the truth.

Hattie Devereaux, her friend and confidante and the sweetest, most stubborn woman to ever maneuver a pirogue down the bayou, was really *dead.*

"No," she whispered. Hattie had always been there for Julie, telling her everything would be all right. She'd been there when Julie was alone and pregnant and in desperate need of a friend. When she was in the midst of excruciating labor pains. When she held her son in her arms for the very first time, frantically counting all his fingers and toes.

Hattie had always been there when Julie needed her. She'd offered advice and support and guidance and protection. Yes, Hattie had protected her on more than one occasion, and she'd gone to her grave doing just that.

Julie closed her eyes and in her mind heard the phone ring once again. She'd just put Thomas to bed for his afternoon nap and settled herself on the couch with a stack of magazines and the Saturday paper. She'd answered the phone, first snatching up Thomas, who'd been awakened by the noise and had started to cry.

Hattie's voice had carried over Thomas's tired wail. The old woman's words had been barely discernable, so soft and pained and desperate.

"He found me," Hattie whispered. *"They want the locket, Julie...the locket."*

"The locket? But why?" Julie cried.

Hattie didn't seem to be listening. Instead, her breaths came quicker and shorter.

"Hattie, please. Hold on. I'll call 911. I'll—"
There was only silence.

A year and a half of running and hiding and praying, and Julie was no better off than the day she'd learned her husband was working with the mob. She knew Sebastian was hunting her. He wanted to silence her. Once and for all.

But it had been her beloved friend Hattie who'd been silenced. Dear sweet Hattie who'd never had a negative word to say about anybody except old Mr. Peabody, who ran the bait shop on the bayou where she lived. He'd had a pack of dogs that yapped all night and disturbed Hattie's handful of expectant and recovering mothers, and she'd delighted in shaking her broom at him and calling him every colorful name she could think of. Yet at the same time, she'd been the first one to take the old coot a pot full of chicken noodle soup when he'd been stricken with the flu.

She'd had a good heart. That's why Julie had featured the old woman in her "Meet the People" column for the *San Antonio Express-News*. The column had explored the cultural diversity of the city, and when Hattie had come to San Antonio for a brief period to help train midwives in the Mexican community, Julie had done a full story on her. She'd not only written a great piece, but made a great friend in the process.

Now she sat here, hours after receiving Hattie's warning call, still not believing her friend was gone.

"No!" The frantic plea broke from Julie's lips just as glass shattered and an arm reached inside the apartment. A large hand twisted the dead bolt and the door slammed open.

"Get the hell away from her...." Dylan's words faded as he caught sight of her sitting on the floor. Thomas in her arms.

His gaze swept her from head to toe before making a frantic visual search of the surrounding room.

"I—I'm alone," she managed to say, swallowing against the lump in her throat. Her chest hurt and her head ached and her entire body felt as if someone had used her for a punching bag. She forced herself to take another breath and concentrated on banishing the black dots dancing before her eyes.

As if he didn't believe her, he glanced around the room again.

"What happened?"

Julie met Dylan's gaze. "She's dead." With the words came a spill of fresh tears that temporarily blinded her.

She blinked frantically and wiped at her face, but the effort proved useless. The tears kept coming. Hattie was gone and Julie had no doubt that she herself would soon follow. If Sebastian had managed to find the old woman in the heart of the Louisiana bayou, miles away from civilization, tracing Julie's whereabouts wouldn't be much more difficult.

Especially since Hattie had Julie's cell phone number in her old flower print address book. It wouldn't take long to trace her—not for a man like Sebastian, who had connections.

Mob connections.

Her skin prickled and her heart pounded, her

breath whooshing from her lungs as quickly as she could draw it in.

Not that Julie feared for herself. She worried over Thomas and what would become of him should something happen to her.

Blood meant nothing to Sebastian. He knew he had a son by now, but all that mattered to him was money and power, and anyone who stood in the way of either, including his infant, would be eliminated if need be.

Julie told herself that, but she hadn't really believed it until now. Until she'd listened to Hattie draw her last breath at the hands of Sebastian's men.

A sob pushed past her lips a heartbeat before she felt him. Muscular arms reached for her and pulled her close and she found herself enveloped in the strong, secure warmth that was Dylan Garrett.

It was an embrace she'd felt many times over the past ten years. Back at Texas A & M when she'd been particularly frustrated over a poor test score. In the first year of her marriage when she'd been lonely because Sebastian had been working long hours and spending less and less time with her. In the past few months when she'd been particularly frightened because the man she married, the man she'd thought she'd loved, had become her pursuer.

Sebastian. A criminal. A murderer.

She shivered and Dylan's arms tightened. For the next few moments, the cold gripping her eased and the future didn't look quite as grim.

That's the way it always was with Dylan. He made her feel safe and protected and loved. Not loved as in till death do us part. He loved her like a friend, just as Hattie loved her.

The way Hattie *had* loved her, but the old woman was gone now. *Dead.*

Because of Julie.

"I want you to take a deep breath and calm down." Dylan's words came from far away, pushed past the pounding of her heart and drew her away from the terror that held her captive. And the grief.

"Julie? Can you hear me?" He spoke again and the reality of his voice sent a calming warmth through her.

"I...yes," she managed with quivering lips.

She did as he instructed and finally the sobs subsided. She swallowed and wiped at her cheeks. "I'm sorry. It's just that I never expected... I mean, I did expect it. I knew it. I knew what he was capable of. That's why I left, why I've been running, but deep down I guess I never thought he would actually go that far. I didn't really believe it.'' Her gaze lifted and locked with his. ''But she's dead, Dylan.'' She bit her lip against another bout of tears. ''Hattie's dead and it's my fault.''

''First off, it's not your fault.''

''I led him to her. She helped me and he found her and killed her because of it and there was nothing I could do to stop it—''

''Hold on,'' he interrupted her. ''I want you to slow down, start at the beginning and tell me everything. And forget the blame. It's not your fault.'' He said the words with such conviction that Julie almost believed them. Except she knew better. If Hattie hadn't been her friend, hadn't helped her during a time when she'd had nothing and no one, the old woman would be alive right now.

''She wanted to help you. It was her choice. She knew the danger involved.''

''How could she when I really didn't? I mean, intellectually I knew Sebastian was capable of this, but in my heart I never truly believed it.''

''No one did.''

''I should have. I heard for myself that day

in his office what sort of man he was. He's involved with the mob, for heaven's sake. I should have known what he'd be capable of.''

"What's done is done. We can't change it. We can only deal with the situation now, which is why I want you to tell me everything. We have to know what we're up against.''

"What *I'm* up against," she corrected. "This isn't your fight, Dylan. You shouldn't be here right now. It's too dangerous. I know I called you, but I panicked. I—''

"This is my fight. You need help. So stop beating yourself up and tell me what happened. From start to finish.''

Julie drew in a deep breath and forced her thoughts back in time, to the moment she'd sat down on the couch. She told him about the phone ringing, about Thomas waking up and the dread in her stomach when she'd heard Hattie's words.

He found me. They want the locket, Julie...the locket.

As Julie told Dylan about Hattie's labored breathing and then the silence, she watched as the concern on his face faded into nothing short of pure rage.

"She did her best," Julie finished. "More

than her best to keep my whereabouts safe, but he found the cell phone number, I'm sure of it. He probably knows where I am right now.''

"Maybe," Dylan said. "But I doubt Sebastian was at Hattie's—he would have sent hired thugs. He wouldn't risk his own cover."

At one time, the reality would have sent a full-blown panic through her, but she was tired. So tired.

And mad, she quickly realized.

The anger rolled through her and she embraced it, letting it fill her with a new sense of determination—a strange emotion to a woman who'd spent the past year afraid of anyone and everything.

Fear had kept her running all this time. Fear for her son's life. For her own.

The thing was, neither she nor Thomas really had a life.

The realization came as she sat there on the apartment floor, with Dylan next to her, and Hattie's last words ringing in her ears. They hadn't been living at all. Merely existing. Surviving. Just when she settled in one spot and established some sense of normalcy, something happened and off she went looking for the next safe place. When she found it, the pattern started all over again.

Thanks to Sebastian.

In the name of money, he'd robbed her and her son of their home, their security, their identity, their future. Now he'd taken Hattie from them, and there was only one thing Julie could do about it.

What she should have done in the first place.

"He's not coming after me this time," she said with more determination than she'd felt in a long time.

But then he'd finally pushed her to the edge. Julie Cooper had reached her limit. It was the end of the line. Time for action rather than reaction.

"He sure as hell isn't," Dylan growled, "because you're getting out of here. Now. I know just the place—"

She shook her head. "I didn't mean that. I meant that he's not coming after me because I'm beating him to the punch."

"What are you talking about?"

She gathered her courage and drew it around her like a protective shield. Her gaze met Dylan's. "*I'm* going after *him*."

CHAPTER TWO

"YOU'RE DOING *what?*" Dylan stared at Julie and tried to comprehend what she'd just said.

"You heard me. I'm going after him. I'm putting a stop to all of this." Her gaze lifted from the child resting in her arms. "I can't do it anymore."

"You can't do what? Stay alive? Because that's what you're doing right now. You're surviving and you're keeping your son safe."

"Safe?" She shook her head. "Like Hattie? She was as far removed from San Antonio as she could get. Lord, she was miles from civilization. Her place is far back in the swamp and he still found her. And he'll find me. He'll find *us.*" She stared down at the small boy in her arms and touched his chubby cheek.

The sight sent a rush of warmth through Dylan. He loved to watch her look at Thomas, touch him, trace the outline of his perfect little ear with the very tip of her finger.

It wasn't fair that the little boy's whole life had been a secret from the start.

"I won't run anymore. I won't live in fear of the day he'll burst through that door the way you just did. I know what he's capable of now." A tear slid from the corner of her eye and wound a path down her cheek.

Dylan felt the urge to reach out and catch the drop, to touch his own fingertip to her closed eyelids and erase all the bad things she'd been forced to endure, and it took all his effort to resist.

But he did.

He had to. Old habits died hard, and Dylan had been resisting his feelings for Julie far too long to change now. Besides, with the powerful emotion roiling inside him, he was desperately afraid he'd do something he would surely regret.

Like pull her into his arms and kiss her until she went all soft against him.

But right now he had to talk some sense into her.

"Are you crazy?" he demanded. "You can't just sit here and wait for those guys to catch up."

"I'm not going to."

"Good," he said, relief rushing through him. A feeling that was short-lived when he heard her next words.

"I'm going after him."

"You are crazy."

"Actually, I feel pretty sane." She gave him a shaky smile and he was reminded of the time they'd gone bungy jumping during spring break. She'd been so determined to do something daring, to live life in the fast lane as she'd dubbed it time and time again.

Anything had been fast compared with her calm, sheltered upbringing in Wisconsin. As the daughter of a dairy farmer, the most excitement she'd seen during her youth was weekly sing-alongs at the local church.

Julie had been determined to try everything she'd been missing, and she'd spent college doing just that. Accumulating new experiences to make up for lost time. Trying her hand at any and everything, no matter how difficult. She'd been determined and totally in awe of life.

He'd always loved that about her.

Hell, he'd loved everything. He still did, and she didn't have so much as a clue.

"In fact," she went on, "this is the sanest I've felt in a long time. I've got a plan."

"I don't think I want to hear this."

"Hattie mentioned something about the locket I gave her. It was a gift from my mother, and it was all I had to give her as payment for taking such good care of Thomas and me. She said the men wanted it." Her gaze collided with his. "Why?"

"Damned if I know."

"Me, either." She shook her head. "But I'm going to find out."

"You're going to get yourself into a mess of trouble."

"I'm already in trouble. And so is Thomas. And so are you." Her gaze went to his bleeding knuckles, courtesy of the smashed window. As if the wound seemed to register for the first time, she started to get up. "I've got a first-aid kit—"

"Forget it. It's fine. Let's finish this. You're not going after Sebastian."

"I am," she said, ignoring his words and climbing to her feet. She placed Thomas on the floor and retrieved the kit from the bathroom. Settling on the couch, she patted the seat next to her and motioned him over.

"You're not," he said again, gritting his teeth and standing his ground.

"I have to." She waved a bottle of antibiotic cream at him. "You're not safe. Neither is anyone else who's ever had the misfortune to know me. Don't you see? It has to come to an end sooner or later. I'm just speeding things up by facing the situation now." Her gaze locked with his again. "I'm going back to Hattie's to find that locket."

"What if Hattie misunderstood? What if the locket doesn't mean a damned thing?"

"What if it does?"

Dylan knew as he took in her stubborn expression, determination glittering in her eyes, that no matter what he said, it would not be enough to keep her from heading to Louisiana. She was going to waltz into the lion's den.

And damned if he was going to allow her to do it without him.

He drew in a deep breath, crossed the room, sank down onto the couch next to her and held out his bleeding hand.

"All right then. Louisiana, here we come."

HE WAS GOING to make her pay.

Sebastian Cooper slammed the phone down and bolted to his feet. He paced the length of his posh office located in the heart of downtown

San Antonio and damned himself for letting someone else handle the situation for him.

He should have been the one to question the dying old woman. He would have gotten the truth out of her one way or another before she croaked.

Sebastian always got what he wanted.

But it was too late now. The stubborn old woman was dead and he was no closer to finding the locket.

Thanks to his dear, sweet, pain-in-the-ass wife.

She'd given the old bat the locket in the first place.

Sebastian rubbed his throbbing temples. Of course, that hadn't started the permanent headache he'd been nursing for more than a year. Julie's running away had done that.

She'd up and disappeared and he'd been worried. He'd had to be worried. Everyone had expected it of him. Truthfully, she'd inconvenienced him more than anything. He'd had two charity functions the following weekend and she'd been expected to attend with him.

He'd managed to save face, but he hadn't forgiven her.

His temples pounded all the harder and bitterness welled inside him. His throat burned and his fingers itched to slide around her throat and squeeze.

At first, he'd been merely interested in the locket. If Julie didn't want to do her duty as Mrs. Sebastian Cooper, he could easily find someone else. But as time had progressed, his headaches had intensified and his anger had stirred.

He pictured Julie's face and heat surged through him. Now he not only wanted the locket back, he wanted to punish her for causing so much trouble.

For listening in when she'd had no right. His business was *his* business.

She'd overheard too much and she'd left. He knew that now. But when she disappeared he'd had to call in the cops. Having the cops digging around could have caused him trouble.

But all that would soon be over. While he didn't have the locket, his men had learned Julie's cell phone number and had tracked her down.

She was living in the tiny little town of Boot Hill, probably sporting a different hair color, not to mention using an alias. Julie and her baby.

He thought briefly of the child, but he didn't feel any of the soft emotions most fathers felt. Sebastian hadn't gotten to where he was by being soft. It took guts and an iron will to run a financial consulting business as ruthless and successful as his. The competition was fierce, but Cooper Consulting had still climbed to the top of the hill and stayed there for the past several years. Thanks to Sebastian's head for numbers and his competitive edge.

Even in the early days, when his company had been small and insignificant, he hadn't hesitated to go head-to-head with the big boys. He'd played hard and pushed them all out of the ring, determined to be the only one left standing. *The* force when it came to business consulting. The king of the hill.

He'd succeeded.

Sebastian always succeeded, and while he still hadn't found the locket, he wasn't going to let defeat get the best of him. He *would* find it, and then his worries would be over.

J. B. Crowe, notorious crime boss, was the only thing standing in Sebastian's way when it came to controlling the illegal businesses operating in the San Antonio area. He was serving time now, but what Sebastian had on him would lock him behind bars for the rest of his life. And Luke Silva, his right-hand man, would be there by his side.

Then Sebastian would step up and take control.

Control. That's what it was all about. He liked being the one in power. The boss.

Julie had escaped him for a little while, but Sebastian was on to her now.

He stared at the address he'd written on his notepad and smiled.

Yes, he was on to her, all right.

"I REALLY DON'T think this is a good idea." Julie stood in the doorway and glanced around the inside of the small motel room.

A double bed filled most of the space, flanked by two scarred nightstands. A small table and two chairs sat near the doorway. With the psychedelic-patterned bedspread and the green shag carpet, it wasn't exactly luxury accommodation. But then she hadn't expected much more when they'd pulled into the parking lot of the Boxcar Inn, the only motel in Willis, Texas. Willis was a desperately small town smack-dab between San Antonio and Houston and the last place Julie had expected Dylan to stop.

That was the trouble in a nutshell. Not the limited accommodations, but the fact that Julie didn't need accommodations.

She needed to keep driving.

She turned toward him. "We can't stay here."

"This is the only room they had." He kicked the door shut behind him and tossed his keys to the small table. "You and Thomas can take the bed. I'll be fine in one of these chairs."

"I didn't mean *here*. I meant here—this place, this town. We should keep moving."

"We need to sleep."

"We can sleep in the car. We'll take turns driving."

"Real sleep," he said. "In a real bed."

"But the car is fine. Actually, the front seat looks bigger than this bed. Probably more comfortable, too." She turned back toward him just in time to see the light that flashed in his eyes.

Pleasure.

"A double's all they had. Don't worry." He winked. "I'm not plotting anything other than a few hours of sleep. You're safe with me." He shrugged off his jacket. "I'll just bunk out in one of these chairs."

"I know I'm safe with you, and you can forget about sleeping in a chair. This bed is plenty big for all of us." At her words, the strange glimmer faded and his mouth tightened, as if she'd disappointed him somehow.

Crazy. She was definitely exhausted and seeing things. Why would Dylan be disappointed at the notion of a soft mattress?

Before she could contemplate the question, he added, "I need a shower. A cold shower," he muttered. "Unless you want the bathroom first?"

She shook her head and tried to ignore the strange tingle in her nipples at the sight of his large hands fingering change. *Punchy and delusional.*

Even so, he really did have nice hands, his fingers long and tanned and—

"If Sebastian's men are on our trail," she blurted, anxious to derail her train of thought from the path it was taking, "it seems foolish to slow down, don't you think?"

"They'd be coming from Louisiana. They'll be expecting you to run the other way, *away* from them. They won't figure you crazy enough to head straight for them.''

''Or smart enough.'' She *was* doing the smart thing. She knew that, felt it deep in her bones. The knowledge was all that kept her from sinking to her knees with Thomas in her arms and crying her eyes out over all the things that had gone wrong in her life.

She'd done that too many times and it hadn't helped a bit. But this…this would solve things.

That's what she told herself, what she believed.

Right now, that is.

But if she gave herself time to think, she feared that the doubts she'd left behind in Boot Hill would surely catch up to her. The grief. The sheer terror.

She glanced down as Thomas squirmed and whined softly in her arms. He looked tired, his eyes heavy-lidded. But they wouldn't close. They hadn't closed since the telephone had startled him awake back in the apartment, and the following chaos—her cries, the window breaking, Dylan's shout, the roar of the Jeep engine as they'd sped away—had kept him awake.

Thomas needed the bed, the quiet, the calm, and so Julie drew in a deep breath and sank down on the edge of the mattress. Kicking off her shoes, she inched back until her shoulders leaned against the headboard. She gathered her son close, his face nestled against the curve of her neck, and rested her head on the soft down of his hair.

A deep breath and the sweet scent of baby powder and innocence filled her nostrils, and her heart slowed its frantic pace. Everything fell away for a few moments as she closed her eyes and crooned softly to him.

There was no Sebastian. No danger. No uncertain future. Just the soft sound of Thomas's breathing and the warmth of his small body.

"Here." The low murmur of Dylan's voice drew her eyes open in time to see him place the gun on the bed next to her.

Shiny gray metal gleamed in the dim lamplight. "I thought you said we were safe for now."

"Just in case." He stared down at her for a long moment and she had the strange urge he wanted to tell her something. That, or he waited to hear something.

"The bed really is plenty big," she said. The notion of him cramped in a chair bothered her more than she would have guessed. "We've already inconvenienced you enough."

"Don't answer the door," he barked before turning away and checking to make sure the locks were secure.

The enormity of their situation hit her as she lay there, the gun beside her, and watched Dylan peer past the tightly drawn drapes.

The muscles in his forearms bunched tight with every movement and she noted the tense set of his shoulders, the severe line of his mouth.

A memory rushed at her and she remembered him in the exact same pose, only he wore a smile on his face as he stared past the drapes to see if Sebastian had reached the front walk.

She'd planned a surprise party for his twenty-first birthday and Dylan had helped her.

He'd always helped. Whether she needed his assistance on a particularly grueling Spanish paper or when she'd needed an extra hand to move her furniture into her very first apartment after the dorm.

Whatever the situation, he'd been there.

Just as he was now, despite the danger that waited on the other side of the door.

"Thank you," she whispered, the words tangling in the sudden lump that formed in her throat.

"What did you say?"

She cleared her throat. "I said thank you. For helping me." Her gaze dropped to Thomas. "For helping us."

"Forget it."

"You're a good person, Dylan. My hero." She'd meant the words as a compliment, but they didn't draw the usual smile from his lips. Instead, his frown deepened, and for the second time in all of fifteen minutes, Julie had the impression she'd said the wrong thing.

"Try to get some sleep," he muttered as he turned the dead bolt and slid the chain. With the locks in place, he strode into the bathroom and closed the door behind him. A few seconds later, the shower started to run, and Julie was left to wonder what she'd done wrong.

Everything.

She'd married the wrong man. Wasted too many years on a one-sided marriage. Put her only child in the pathway of danger. And now she'd disrupted Dylan's life. Again.

"Not for long," she murmured to Thomas, more determined than ever to put an end to things. For so long she'd run because of

Thomas. To keep him safe. To keep him away from Sebastian.

But the only way to do that was to keep Sebastian away from him. Permanently. And the only way to do that was to expose him once and for all.

The vow made her think again of the small locket she'd given Hattie in payment for services rendered. The midwife had helped Julie when she'd been down and out and pregnant and she'd owed her dearly for her help. She'd given her the only possession of worth she had—the gold locket inlaid with a small diamond that her mother had given her years ago.

Sebastian wanted the locket. But why?

She needed to think about the question, but then Thomas cooed and drew her attention and she saw only her precious boy.

Caressing one chubby cheek, she relished the feel of his soft skin and thanked the Powers That Be yet again for blessing her with such an incredible gift.

She'd prayed so many times for a child. The news had been both a blessing and a tragedy since her desire to share the news with Sebastian had led her to his office, where she'd discovered the type of man she'd married—a cold, callous businessman involved in illegal dealings with the mob.

What she'd overheard those few moments in his office had sent her running for her life and that of her unborn son's.

Her gaze went again to the chubby eight-month-old in her arms.

For Thomas she could do this. He needed her, loved her, depended on her, and she had no intention of letting him down. She refused to waste her time worrying. Focus. That was the key to keeping her fears at bay and beating Sebastian in his game of cat and mouse.

Dylan was right. She had to forget the past and concentrate on the present. This moment. And right now, she needed to rebuild her strength.

Determined, she settled back and concentrated on slowing her pounding heart. Oddly enough, it wasn't that difficult. Soon, her body relaxed and the tightness in her chest seeped away. With Thomas warm and snug in her arms and the steady rush of the shower lulling her senses, she didn't feel as nervous about the future. As anxious.

For the first time since she'd gone on the run

and into hiding a year and a half ago, Julie Cooper actually felt safe.

MY HERO.

The soft words echoed through Dylan's mind as he stood next to the bed and stared down at the woman stretched out on her back. She lay with one arm above her head, the other resting softly against her thigh. Her white tank top had ridden up, exposing a few delicious inches of her midriff. The soft cotton molded to her full breasts. Light-brown hair fanned out across the stark white pillow and draped her pale shoulders. Julie was a natural blonde, but she'd dyed her hair brown and worn brown contacts as part of her disguise. To Dylan she was just as beautiful.

His groin tightened, the sight of her simply too much for him to handle. Not when he'd dreamed of her just like this nearly every night since he'd met her.

He snatched up the gun and turned away. Hooking his piece in his waistband, he pulled back the drapes for a quick surveillance.

The motel sign glittered in red neon, casting a glow on the parking lot. Dylan watched as a large, balding man in a Hawaiian print shirt ushered two kids from a station wagon into a nearby room. The door shut behind the man and quiet fell.

There were no strangers lurking about, no unusual cars. Nothing out of the ordinary.

Not that Dylan was about to relax. Years undercover had taught him never to let his guard down. A situation could go from calm to chaotic in the blink of an eye. At the thought he checked the gun for ammunition, shifted the safety to off and settled the firearm down on the table within easy reach.

She'd been right. They should have kept moving. He'd been trying to ease her fear when he'd said that Sebastian's men wouldn't expect them to head in their direction. But Dylan suspected for some time that Sebastian knew he'd found Julie. It wouldn't surprise Dylan if someone had seen them leave Boot Hill and was tracking them now.

Another quick scan of the parking lot and he let the drapes fall back into place. They were damned no matter which direction they ran. Their only hope was to be cautious and stay one step ahead of their pursuers. Which was why he intended to wait before calling his sister Lily to tell her what was up.

Lily was his older sister by a few minutes, a fact she'd held over his head as long as he could remember. That had been her excuse to boss him around when they were kids, and worry over him just as she was probably doing right now.

Since she'd married last year and had baby Elizabeth, she'd been even more protective. No doubt she was frantic after his abrupt departure from Max and Rachel's wedding.

Then again, she knew Dylan. She trusted him. She might worry, but she wouldn't think the worst until she had proof one way or another, which gave him time to come up with a way to contact her without leaving a trail as to his whereabouts.

Sinking down into the chair, Dylan stretched his legs out and readied himself for a watchful night. He'd let Julie drive part of the way in the morning while he caught an hour's nap. It wasn't much time for the average man, but Dylan had cut his teeth on twenty-four-hour stakeouts that required full alertness.

The lack of sleep he could handle. It was the present company he had his doubts about.

He drew in a deep breath and tried to ignore

the call of the soft mattress not more than a few feet away.

There's plenty of room for all of us.

She'd meant the comment to be thoughtful, but all it had done was stick in his craw because sweet Julie hadn't batted an eye at the prospect of him climbing into bed next to her.

He might as well have been her brother.

He wasn't, and the thoughts that pushed into his head were anything but familial. He wanted to climb into bed, pull her into his arms, feel her body soft and warm and rounded against his. He wanted to kiss her, to slip his tongue past her full lips and taste her. He wanted to part her legs and slide deep, deep into her warm, waiting body....

The thought made him harder and hotter and he shifted in the vinyl chair, searching for a comfortable position when the only true relief was putting as much distance as possible between himself and the sleeping woman.

Fat chance. All the time she'd been away from him, he'd thought about her. Dreamed of her. Wanted her.

Lord, he *was* crazy. Loony tunes. Insane. This was Julie, not some glamour queen or luscious centerfold.

His head knew that, but damned if his body was listening.

Water dripped from his still damp hair and slid over his shoulder, down his chest, but it wasn't enough to cool the fire that burned deep inside him, just as an ice-cold shower hadn't been enough.

Hell, a dive straight into the Arctic wouldn't do it.

He wanted her far too much.

But she didn't want him.

My hero.

The truth echoed through his head, stirring his irritation, making him as angry as it did sad, because Dylan didn't want to be her hero.

He wanted to be her partner. Her lover. Her *man.*

He wasn't sure what happened in that next instant, why he suddenly felt the urge to embrace the truth when he'd been ignoring it for the past ten years. Maybe it was the way Rachel and Max had looked so happy and in love at their wedding earlier that day. Maybe it was the sheer terror he'd felt when faced with the possibility of losing Julie forever. Maybe it was the way she'd clung to him, as if he were her only lifeline, while she'd cried for Hattie.

Maybe all three.

Dylan only knew that he couldn't keep denying his feelings a moment longer. He wanted Julie as a man wanted a woman, and he wanted her to want him in exactly the same way.

Soon, he vowed to himself, he would change the way she thought about him.

Dylan shrugged off the damp T-shirt he'd pulled on in the bathroom and tossed it on the table, leaving only his jeans on.

Julie was going to see the real man.

Starting right now.

"I FINALLY GOT a lead.

Luke Silva smiled when he heard the voice come over his speakerphone. Excitement rushed through him, but no one would ever have known. Luke didn't let his feelings show—what little he had, and according to the men he conducted business with, that amounted to zero. A cold sonofabitch. That's what people thought of him. He liked the fact. People didn't mess with a sonofabitch unless they had a death wish.

Sebastian Cooper was as good as dead.

He slid off his dark glasses and set them on the desk before unfastening his bolo tie.

"Boss?" came the voice from the other end of the line. "You there?"

Luke didn't bother answering. He didn't like to waste his words. He believed in action. All bite and no bark, that was his motto.

"Boss?"

"When?"

The one word was enough of a reassurance for Mikey, who'd worked for Silva on several jobs and knew how to conduct himself. He didn't push or run his mouth.

"A few hours ago," Mikey told him. "That tip we got from Cooper's secretary turned out to be the gospel. Sebastian's keeping a low profile right now, using a hired gun to do his dirty work."

"Who?"

"Cap Pendleton."

Luke smiled. Cooper was weak, but smart. He'd hired one of the best.

But Luke was better. A crack shot, and he intended to prove it where Sebastian Cooper was concerned. One shot and it would all be over.

"I didn't even recognize him at first," Mikey continued. "I've never seen a guy so good at blending into the woodwork. He's right there in your face, but you don't even know it."

"Has anyone else recognized him?"

"Not yet. Garrett's good, but he's preoccupied right now with Cooper's wife and the baby. He's looking over his shoulder, but he doesn't see anything. I think he senses something, though. It's the ex-cop in his blood."

"Stay close to Pendleton but not too close. I just want you to watch him right now. If we give him time, he'll lead us to Cooper."

"Sure thing, boss."

Luke punched the off button on the speaker-phone and smiled. It was just a matter of time before he gave Sebastian Cooper what was coming to him. Luke didn't like being pushed aside, and Cooper had tried to do just that. Luke had worked too hard to get where he was at. He was *made*, damn it! In the grand scheme of things, *made* men were at the top of the food chain. If Cooper thought he could just shoulder his way in and grab a seat he hadn't earned, he had another think coming.

Crowe might have put up with it because Cooper had a brain behind his greed and J.B. liked his money-making skills. But J.B. was out of the picture at the moment. Luke was running things now, and while he was careful to carry out J.B.'s orders, this was one situation where Luke himself was calling the shots.

He'd spit on the devil before he let a snot-nose punk like Cooper jockey for a powerful position he hadn't earned. Things didn't work that way in Silva's world. It wasn't just about smarts. It was about balls.

Luke wouldn't have bothered to use a hired gun to clean up his dirty laundry. He liked doing it himself, which was why he had Mike simply watching.

Luke liked the killing. He always had—when he was back in Mexico City, giving it to some street punk trying to screw him out of a few pesos, and now as he sat in his twenty-bedroom mansion in The Dominion, San Antonio's most elite neighborhood, and handed down orders to his subordinates. He was still the one to pull out his Glock 9mm and maintain order.

He was a long way from Reynosa, his home long forgotten. But he hadn't forgotten what had brought him so far.

There were rules to follow. An order to things. Anyone who disrupted that order and threatened his livelihood had to be punished. Sebastian Cooper wasn't playing by the rules, and so Luke would take particular pleasure in putting the man in his rightful place—six feet under.

Just as soon as he managed to corner him.

CHAPTER THREE

JULIE NEVER wanted to wake up.

She sighed, clamping her eyes tight against the morning light that spilled past the edge of the drapes. The dream was much better than reality and so she struggled to hold on to it a few precious minutes more.

In the hazy warmth of sleep, she imagined strong arms holding her close, tight against a hard chest. A strong, steady heartbeat echoed through her head and mimicked her own. A musky male scent filled her nostrils and she inhaled, drawing the fragrance deeper, letting it fill her senses.

Mmm...

The rustle of blankets followed by a gurgling *coo* pushed past the sleepy fog and shattered the last remnants of her dream.

She opened her eyes to the double bed covered in cheap white sheets and a psychedelic orange comforter. Her gaze shifted to Thomas, who stirred beside her, his fist waving wildly before finding its way to his mouth.

He chewed his fingers, drool trailing from the corner of his mouth, and gurgled a few more unintelligible sounds.

I'm hungry. That's what he was saying in a language mothers were built to understand.

Julie sighed and threw off the covers. She'd used up most of the food she'd hurriedly packed the night before. A quick rummage through her purse left her with an empty bag of animal crackers and a half-eaten jar of baby food.

"I don't think this is any good, Thomas."

The baby waved his fist and let out a fussy whine. Julie had about five seconds to find something for breakfast before all hell broke loose. At least she had the ready-mixed cans of formula she'd brought along.

She dug up a handful of change from the bottom of her purse. Not enough for the vending machines she'd spotted outside on their way in the night before. Not that they'd have much for a baby, anyway.

Thomas gave another frantic wave of his fist and a loud cry. "Hold on, baby." Popping his pacifier into his eager mouth, she pulled her tennis shoes from beneath the bed, slipped them on and stood.

Two steps and Julie stopped cold, her gaze riveted on Dylan and the picture he made lounging in the chair, his cowboy hat tipped low on his head. He wore nothing but jeans, his long feet bare, propped on another chair and hooked at the ankles. A faint snore filled the room and she realized he was asleep.

And half-naked.

The truth echoed in her head as her gaze shifted to his bare chest. Dark, silky swirls of hair spread from nipple to nipple, then narrowed into a funnel that dipped beneath the waistband of his jeans. His shoulders were broad, his arms heavily muscled, as if he spent his time doing hard labor rather than P.I. work.

He *did* do hard labor, she reminded herself. He divided his time between Finders Keepers, the private investigation firm he ran with his sister, Lily, and the Double G, his family's ranch just outside of San Antonio. Dylan Garrett could ride and rope and cowboy as well as any of the paid hands at the Double G. She'd seen him on the back of a horse the few times she'd been out to the ranch. Watched his expertise as he maneuvered the reins and went after a rowdy calf. Enjoyed the full-blown grin that had curved his lips when he'd broken a particularly ornery horse.

But in all the years she'd known him, she'd never seen him like this.

So hard and muscular and...*sexy*.

You're not some naive virgin, she reminded herself. *You've seen men before.*

Sebastian was buff and tanned and very attractive. The sight of Dylan shouldn't be anything out of the ordinary.

Her head knew that, yet her heart continued to hammer. Her blood rushed. Her nerves buzzed.

The urge to reach out and run her fingers through his chest hair, trace the contours of every muscle, feel the steady thump of his pulse against the pad of her finger, was nearly overwhelming.

This was Dylan, she reminded herself. Her buddy, her pal. She shouldn't be having such thoughts about him, particularly since he didn't have similar thoughts about her.

Nothing but friendship.

They'd spent plenty of time together over the years, and never once had he made a pass. He'd always been a perfect gentleman. Someone she could trust.

A friend.

She knew that, and still her body responded to his. Called to his. Begged for his. As if he were more to her.

Because she wanted him to be more.

Her hand moved forward and she reached out, stopping just shy of actually making any contact, thanks to Thomas, who chose that moment to coo.

Heavens, what was she thinking?

She wasn't thinking, period. Obviously a few hours' sleep hadn't done anything to help her state of mind. She was still punchy. Irrational.

Scared.

The fear accounted for her racing heart. Fear and anxiety and the need to get on with things. That along with the fact that Dylan Garrett was one good-looking male specimen and she was a red-blooded female.

A tired female at that. Coupled with the fact that she'd always found Dylan handsome, that she'd even fantasized about him on occasion, it was no wonder her body was experiencing such a response.

She wasn't surprised, but she was dismayed.

The timing was all wrong, not to mention Dylan was off-limits. Julie knew all too well what happened when friends took their relationship a step further. If things didn't work out, it wasn't merely a romance lost, but a friendship. And Julie valued Dylan's far too much to take such a risk on account of lust.

And that's all it was. He was handsome. She was a fully functional woman who'd been celibate too many months to count. It made sense.

But this wasn't the time or the place, and certainly not the man. She wouldn't ruin the special closeness she shared with Dylan by making advances toward him.

On that note, Julie forced her attention past him to the pile of change sitting on the table. Grabbing a few quarters, she moved toward the door and reached for the lock.

A loud *click* filled the room as the dead bolt turned. In a heartbeat, Julie found herself shoved up against the door, a hard wall of solid muscle pressing into her back.

"Where do you think you're going?" The words were low and deep, rumbling through her ear and making her heart pound even faster.

She drew in a deep, steadying breath and

tried to ignore the man behind her, surrounding her, pressing into her.

Pressing?

Yes, he was definitely pressing. Not hard, mind you. Just enough so that she couldn't move.

She could only breathe. And feel.

Heavens, could she feel.

The hard wall of his chest at her back. The warmth of his breath against the bare curve of her neck. The firm cradle of his hips against her buttocks. The solid feel of his legs flanking hers.

"You shouldn't be going outside. Especially not when you think I'm asleep."

"I didn't want to wake you. I…" Julie licked her suddenly dry lips and drew in a shaky breath. "Thomas is hungry and—" she gave a quick flick of her tongue across her bottom lip "—so am I."

Boy, was she ever.

She forced the notion aside and concentrated on taking deep, measured breaths. A bad move, because his scent now filled her head as well, skimmed her nerve endings, coaxed her body to life.

This is Dylan, remember? Your friend. Your best friend.

"I saw vending machines over by the stairwell when we checked in." She ducked beneath his arm and sidestepped away. "I have formula but I wanted to see if there was any apple juice or plain cookies."

"We'll go to a supermarket."

"That's what I had in mind, but in the meantime…" Thomas chose that moment to let loose a loud wail. "Looks like he's not going to wait any longer. I'll fix a bottle," Julie said.

Dylan grinned, a slight tilt of his lips that sent a surge of warmth through her and made her heart pound faster. "He does sound desperate. I'll go." He pulled his shirt on and tucked the gun into the back waistband of his pants.

"Oh, and see if they have Doritos," Julie said as he pulled the door open and peered outside.

"Doritos? For a baby?" Dylan looked aghast.

"The Doritos are for me," Julie answered him.

He smiled this time. A typical Dylan smile, but it didn't draw the usual response. There was no sense of comfort. No rush of relief. Instead, her heart fluttered and a strange warmth hummed through her body.

Friends, she reminded herself, holding fast to the knowledge.

"Lock the door behind me," he finally said, turning away and stepping outside.

Julie hurried over to her bag to get Thomas a fresh diaper and prepare his bottle. While she changed the baby, she tried to make some sense out of what had just happened.

She'd responded to Dylan Garrett. His closeness. His masculinity. *Him.*

Despite the fact that he was her friend. Despite the fact that they were in a dangerous situation and she should be totally and completely focused on staying alive.

The thing was, Dylan made her feel alive. More than she'd ever felt before. He made her heart pound and her blood rush.

Under any other circumstances, she'd feel guilty. After all, legally she was still a married woman. But in her heart she hadn't been married since she'd thrown her rings into that Dumpster a year and a half ago—the day she'd learned the truth about the man she'd married.

What a mess her life had become.

She'd been so certain of Sebastian's love, of his character, and she'd been dead wrong. The love she'd felt for him had died along with her illusions.

She had learned from her mistakes. No way would she risk her friendship with Dylan over a temporary case of lust. Dylan was too good a man to lose.

DYLAN POPPED two quarters into the archaic-looking vending machine and squinted against the early morning sunlight.

Exhaustion tugged at him. He slid a hand around his neck and squeezed, feeling the pull of muscle and tendon. He was tired and uptight and damned happy.

He grinned, remembering the feel of Julie's hair trailing across his chest when she'd leaned over him to pick up the spare change. More than that, it was the look in her eyes when he'd opened his and stared up at her.

Desire.

There'd been no mistaking the fierce glitter of her gaze, or the way she'd licked her lips as if she'd wanted to taste him as badly as he'd wanted to taste her.

But he'd seen surprise as well, and he knew

the emotion he stirred was unfamiliar to her, and so the desire had faded as quickly as it had sparked.

If it had been there in the first place.

He ignored the nagging doubt. Success was all about being positive. About staying focused on the objective and ignoring the small deterrents along the way.

"But I want to go to the pool *now*." The child's voice drew Dylan from his thoughts. He realized in a heartbeat that the man and the two small kids he'd seen the night before stood not three feet away.

Dylan hadn't even heard their approach. He'd been too lost in his thoughts.

"I already told you," the man said, exasperation in his voice. "We'll go after breakfast."

"But that's too long."

"And it's only going to get longer if you don't stop bothering me and let me get your mother's Diet Coke." His words met with a lot of grumbling. "Now get back in the room and watch cartoons." He shrugged as he came up next to Dylan. "Little woman can't function without her morning caffeine."

"I know the feeling." Dylan swiped his own tired eyes and pictured an extra-large cup of steaming black coffee from the nearest convenience store.

"Long night?" the man asked as Dylan stepped to the side and started to feed quarters into the snack machine.

"You could say that." As he leaned down to retrieve a package of vanilla wafers—the only cookies the machine offered—the hair on the back of his neck tingled. Awareness skittered down his spine and he turned.

A man stood across the parking lot in an open motel room doorway. He took a drag off the cigarette in his hands before his gaze collided with Dylan's.

Dylan expected the man to look away as most people did when caught staring, but he didn't. He held Dylan's gaze for a few long moments before flicking the butt of his cigarette and turning to disappear into his room.

"You and the little woman on vacation?" The man next to him fed more quarters into the neighboring machine and retrieved a third diet soda. "I saw you checking in last night," he said by way of explanation. "You and your wife?"

"Um, yeah."

"Vacation?" the man prodded as Dylan's

gaze drifted back to the closed motel room door behind which the stranger had disappeared.

"Yeah," he said. "We're out doing a little sightseeing. Off to see family. How about you?"

"I agreed to AstroWorld in lieu of two weeks with the in-laws from hell." As the two small kids started to punch each other at his side, he shook his head. "I'm actually starting to rethink the decision."

Dylan winked before letting his gaze slide back across the parking lot, to the black Suburban parked in front of the door where the other man had been standing. He made a mental note of the license-plate number.

"...all the way to Florida. We've only been gone a few days, and already the wife's laid up with a massive migraine and I'm getting there. That's why we're here. We were going to drive all the way through to Houston and Six Flags yesterday, but then the wife started getting that familiar pounding and bam, we're cooped up in motel hell with a bag full of greasy burgers and two kids that are driving me nuts."

"Hope the caffeine helps."

"It will, for the wife that is." He struggled with the child clinging to his shorts. "I'm beginning to think the only thing that's going to save me is a noose.''

Dylan grinned before cutting another glance across the parking lot. ''Take it easy.''

''If only.''

A few minutes later, Dylan closed the door behind him and started gathering his stuff off the table.

''We're taking off.''

''What's wrong?'' she asked as she fished a vanilla wafer from the package and gave it to Thomas.

''Nothing. Right now. But we're not sticking around to see that change.''

''Something happened outside.''

''Nothing happened.''

''You saw something?''

Dylan didn't turn toward her. He kept gathering things up and she touched his arm.

''You did see something.''

''More like someone.''

''Sebastian?''

''One of his men. Maybe. I don't want to stick around to find out.''

Panic fired her hazel eyes and Dylan barely resisted the urge to pull her into his arms and swear on his mother's grave that everything

would be all right. That he would let nothing—
no one—hurt her or Thomas.

But she already knew that. He'd pledged as
much time and time again, until he felt like a
damn superhero in her eyes.

No more.

He peeled off his T-shirt and the panic in her
eyes fled. The fire in them burned brighter, hotter. "What are you doing?" she finally blurted,
as if the sight of him undressing bothered her
a lot more than it should have.

"Changing shirts. I always keep spare
clothes in my trunk. Thank God. Otherwise I'd
still be in my tux from yesterday."

"That's not what I mean. Why are you
changing shirts here? There's a bathroom."

"I don't need the bathroom. I just need a
fresh shirt. Does this bother you?"

"Of course not." She cleared her throat.

He grinned as he slid on the shirt, enjoying
the way her gaze seemed riveted on his chest.

"Are you okay?"

"What?"

"I said are you okay?"

"No." She shook her head and her gaze collided with his. "I—I mean of course I'm fine.
Or I will be just as soon as we get on the road."

She turned and started stuffing clothes into her duffel bag.

"We'll hit a supermarket to pick up a few things for Thomas, and grab a coffee for us." He checked his gun and jammed it back into the back waistband of his pants, his expression serious now. "We've got a long ride ahead."

CHAPTER FOUR

IT WAS THE longest ride of Julie's life.

She tried to tell herself it was because of the anxiety that built in the pit of her stomach as they neared Louisiana. But in reality, it had more to do with the man seated only inches across the seat from her.

The closeness of his body had made her catch her breath on more than one occasion, a reaction she hid by clearing her throat and shifting in her seat. That, or turning to eye Thomas, who sat in the back seat, his head limp against the side of the car seat, eyes closed, chest rising slow and steady with each deep breath.

Thomas was enough to distract her for a few seconds as she contemplated how far her son had come in such a short time. At birth, he'd been small, a victim of a stressful pregnancy spent on the run without regular prenatal care.

But visiting an OB-GYN hadn't been an option for Julie when she had been running for her life. She'd been more concerned with survival, and so she'd only managed an occasional checkup here and there at various clinics. Hattie had been her guardian angel. It had taken Julie a long time to track down her old friend, but Hattie had welcomed her immediately. She would have let Julie stay even after Thomas was born, but Julie had been so afraid Sebastian would find her there. Sadly she'd been right, but Hattie had been the one to pay.

Although Sebastian's betrayal had shaken Julie to the very core, she had not lost her faith in the goodness of most people. There had been Hattie, of course, and Justin Dale, the physician in Cactus Creek who had cared for Thomas when he developed pneumonia. It was hard to believe he'd been such a sick baby. At eight months he was thriving, his cheeks had taken on a rosy tinge and his arms and legs filled out to a pleasing plumpness.

And then of course there was Dylan.

Gratitude and friendship. That's what she felt for Dylan. Or what she should have felt as she sat there next to him with barely six inches of upholstery separating them.

Not the heat. The pull. The attraction.

He really was good-looking. He had short,

sun-streaked brown hair and piercing blue eyes. The soft white cotton of his shirt stretched across his broad chest and banded his muscled biceps. A sprinkling of dark hair covered his forearms, and his muscles flexed as he drummed his fingertips on the steering wheel. Her attention shifted to his hands, so large and tanned, his fingers long. Strong.

Before she drew her next breath, the image hit her. Those long, firm fingers dancing across her skin, touching, stroking—

"Penny for your thoughts."

His deep, rumbling voice shattered her thoughts and her gaze jumped to his. Guilt flooded her and heat rose to her cheeks.

"I, um, nothing," she finally muttered. A million wouldn't be enough to force a confession.

She might not be able to suppress her thoughts, but she still had the small consolation that he wasn't aware of what was racing through her mind.

Or was he?

He stared at her a moment longer, and she could have sworn that he saw everything she was thinking, felt what she was feeling.

The same heat. The same pull. The same attraction.

Crazy.

"So do you think we're being followed?"

"It's a possibility." He shook his head. "I still don't get it."

"Get what?"

"How Sebastian could have ended up in the mob. Hell, he was my best friend. How could I miss the real man all those years?"

"I keep asking myself the same question. But we were so young back when we met—so naive. The three of us had such good times. The only hint I ever had was Sebastian's head-on approach to life. He was fearless."

"Hell," Dylan said, "he wasn't afraid of anything. Dare the devil. That was Sebastian."

"Daring the devil, and winning. The winning was what was important to Sebastian. He had to win. At all costs." Her gaze shifted to his profile. "If I'm really honest, I have to admit he didn't fall in love with me. He fell in love with the challenge."

"He loved you, Julie."

"Maybe a part of him did, but it wasn't real love. Not the till-death-do-us-part kind." She stared in front of her, at the endless expanse of highway stretched before them. "It was young love. Infatuation. Temporary. He made me feel smart and beautiful. I'd never met anyone like him. Or you." Now why had she said that?

But it was true. Dylan had been just as handsome, as attentive, as alive as Sebastian.

But he hadn't been pushy. He'd been patient and kind.

She focused on the thought rather than the way his palm guided the steering wheel as he kept the Jeep on course.

"I should have seen him for what he was," Julie admitted.

"You couldn't have. I've known him half my life, yet I don't know him at all. Back when we were teenagers, we'd hook up at the local rodeos and hang out. We both loved horses. Or so I thought, but the more I think about it, the more I realize that it wasn't the horses Sebastian loved so much as the actual competition. The winning. That's what drew him."

"And what drew you?"

He cast her a sideways glance. "The ride, darlin'."

The words conjured another image in her mind, of the two of them, hot and naked and sweaty and—

"You okay?"

What was wrong with her? She was acting like some sex-crazed moron. "Um, yeah," she mumbled. "I'm just hungry." In more ways than one.

Ignoring the last thought, she fixed her attention on a roadside advertisement for a bacon cheeseburger. Her stomach grumbled in response. It had been a long while since breakfast.

"We'll stop." He glanced in the rearview mirror as if looking for something. Or someone. "Pick up some food for the road."

"There's somebody following us?"

He didn't answer her for a long, tense moment. "Maybe," he finally said. He flipped on the turn signal and switched to the right lane. The car cruised onto the exit ramp that led to the feeder road and Billy Bob's Burgers and Beer, a small greasy spoon that sat just off the Interstate. "And maybe not." He pulled into the parking lot and turned into an empty space near the front entrance. "But it's better to assume the worst." He killed the engine.

"The worst being that somebody is trying to catch up with us?"

He leaned over her, his arm brushing her knee as he popped open the glove compartment, retrieved a small handgun and placed it in her trembling hands. "The worst being that some-body's already caught up."

"I DON'T LIKE THIS," Julie said for the tenth time as Dylan held open the door to Billy Bob's.

"It's just a precaution. If I'm not around, you need it for protection."

"What do you mean, if you're not around? Where are you going?"

"The bathroom." He smiled reassuringly and touched the pad of his thumb to her smooth cheek. "If that's okay."

"Okay? I mean, yes, yes, it's okay. For a second I just thought…" She let her words trail off as she shifted the baby to her right hip, her purse hanging securely over her opposite shoul-der. "What if it goes off?"

"The safety's on. You remember how to turn it off?"

"Why shouldn't I? You taught me how to use it. I'm a regular Charlie's Angel."

He grinned. "Supersize my fries."

"I'm armed and dangerous and the man wants fries." She shook her head. "Men."

Dylan left her and Thomas in line behind a

pimply-faced teen and his parents and headed toward the rear of the restaurant. As he walked, he studied the faces surrounding him, from the old man with the handlebar mustache and a giant piece of coconut cream pie on the plate in front of him, to the couple feeding each other bites of chicken-fried steak in the far corner. Nothing out of the ordinary.

Except the pie. Lord, he'd never seen such a large slice. Except at home. His sister had once served him a double slice of chocolate cream pie that would have given Billy Bob's a run for its money. Of course, they'd been ten years old back then and Lily had been anxious to fatten him up after a nasty three-week bout with the flu that had left him five pounds lighter. She'd baked him a pie and brownies and a red velvet cake. Dylan had not only gained ten pounds, but developed a cavity in the process thanks to Lily's mothering.

Speaking of which…

He headed into the men's room and pulled out his cell phone. After punching in a speed-dial number, he listened to the ring on the other end.

"Hello?" A female voice finally floated over the line.

"It's me."

"Dylan?"

"The one and only. Listen," he said, sensing the multitude of questions rolling through her head before she had a chance to voice any. "I don't want to go into detail, for obvious reasons. I don't want you involved in any of this."

"You're my baby brother. I'm involved."

"By eight minutes, and you're not involved, and I'm keeping it that way, so don't worry about where we are." He said the words even though he knew they were useless. Lily would worry because she always worried. They were twins. She was smart, however, and didn't ask their whereabouts.

That, or she couldn't ask.

"You're doing all right, aren't you?"

"As right as Reverend Gabriel after one of his confess-all revival meetings."

The moment he heard the words, he breathed a sigh of relief. If Lily had said yes or okay, he would have known something was wrong. She'd used their phrase from childhood. Their secret code that everything was, indeed, all right.

"Julie and Thomas are with me and we're all okay. For now."

"How's Julie?"

"Strong, as usual. And damned pigheaded."

"What are you talking about?"

"We should be looking for a secure hiding place. Instead, we're going after Sebastian."

He expected several responses, the first along the lines of a frantic *Are you crazy?* Instead, his sister remained silent for a long moment before she finally murmured, "Maybe she's right."

"Are you crazy?" he heard himself demanding.

"The running has got to stop. A baby needs stability. A home and a family."

"I still think this is a bad idea."

"But you're doing it anyway."

"Hell, yes."

"Give Julie my love. Not that she needs it. Not with all you've got directed her way."

Dylan's tone grew serious. "Look after my little niece, okay? And yourself. And call me if you hear anything about Sebastian's whereabouts. I don't care if it's just a rumor."

"You know I will. And you be careful. Otherwise, you won't have Sebastian to worry about. It'll be me coming after you."

He punched the off button and sent up a silent thank you to whoever had invented the cell phone. Otherwise, he never would have been able to call his sister and talk for fear of being traced. But with a cell, the only thing traceable was the phone number. Forget the location.

Of course, there were ways to trace the call if someone had the time and resources. Which is why Dylan intended to keep moving. He had to stay one step ahead of their pursuers.

The slow creak of the door punctuated the thought. He heard the footsteps even before he felt the strange awareness in his gut.

He turned, and that's when he caught sight of the man standing across the room. The same man he'd seen in the doorway of the motel room that morning.

Dylan turned and walked back into the bathroom. A few seconds later, he heard the slow creak of the door as the man followed him.

He caught the guy from behind, whirling him around and shoving him up against the door with a loud thud.

The man groaned. "What the hell are you doing?"

"I think that's my line. Then again, I don't have to ask because I already know. You're following me."

"You're crazy."

"No," Dylan said as he twisted the man's wrist another degree south. "I'm mad. I don't particularly like having to stare over my shoulder every damn second."

"You're paranoid," the man managed. "I'm not—"

"And even worse than being followed," Dylan interrupted, "is being lied to. Are you lying to me?"

"No."

"What?" He twisted harder in a move that had brought many criminals to their knees. This guy was no different.

"Okay," he finally breathed. "But I'm not following you."

"I don't think I heard you."

"I said I'm not following you. I'm after Sebastian's man, and this is strictly a surveillance project. I'm not undercover. I try to keep a low profile."

Sebastian's man? This guy must be working for Luke Silva, who was running the show while the head of the mob, J. B. Crowe, was serving time. Dylan had actually helped get the word out to Crowe that Sebastian was becoming a bit "ambitious," knowing that would guarantee Sebastian's activities were closely observed. He'd hoped that would keep Sebastian off Julie's trail, but it obviously hadn't worked.

"Jeez," the man complained, "would you let go? You're making me lose him."

"Who?"

When the man didn't answer, Dylan twisted again until the guy groaned.

"Who exactly are you following?" Dylan demanded.

"Bite me."

"I'll do better than that." He took out a handcuff and locked it around the man's wrist before attaching the other cuff to the pipe running under the bathroom sink.

"What the hell are you doing?"

"Making sure you stay off our tail."

"For the last time, I'm not following you."

"Tell that to somebody who hasn't been watching you in the rearview mirror for the past ten hours."

"I'm *not*."

The words followed Dylan toward the front of the restaurant where Julie waited, doing her best to juggle two white burger bags, a large soda and a wailing baby.

"What were you doing in there? Reading?"

"Taking care of a little business," he said as he took Thomas in his arms and ushered her out the door.

"Business?" She glanced over her shoulder just as a loud shout came from the rest room. "What are you talking about?"

"I had a little chat with the guy who's been following us," he told her as he steered her into the front of the car and buckled Thomas into his baby seat in the back. "No one's going to be bothering us anymore."

"Guess again." The voice came from behind Dylan a split second before he felt the cold press of metal at the small of his back.

CHAPTER FIVE

JULIE'S GAZE riveted on the knife the stranger held to Dylan's throat, and the soda she'd been holding slipped from her fingers and splattered on the floorboard. Terror welled inside her, rising up, gripping every nerve ending until she could hardly breathe. Her heart thundered and her ears rang and time sucked her back to that dreadful day in Sebastian's office when she'd heard the truth about her husband.

Fear had followed her in her desperate flight, crawled into bed with her at night, smothered her with horrible nightmares of being caught until Dylan had found her six months ago.

Dylan.

She studied his face. There was no flicker of emotion. No tightening of his lips. He looked relaxed, his expression passive. Calm. His gaze was as blue and tranquil as the Caribbean on a hot summer's day. He might well have had a phone pressed to his ear, chitchatting with some friend, rather than a stranger at his back and cold steel pressed to his throat.

"It was you."

Through the fog of terror clogging her brain, Julie heard the deep rumble of his words, and though he couldn't reach out to her and reassure her with his hands as he'd done so many times in the past when she'd been worried or upset or downright scared, he did so with his voice.

I'm here. I'm always here.

She drew in a shaky breath and tried to calm her pounding heart. *Think,* her brain screamed. She needed a way out. A weapon.

Her mind raced frantically for possibilities. She'd tossed her purse, the gun tucked neatly inside, in the back seat next to Thomas. She'd spotted a flashlight in the glove compartment. Some flares. A first-aid kit.

"Yep, it was me, not Mr. Soprano back there. See, he was following me, and I was following you."

"So you don't really have a wife?"

"Sure, I do. And three ex-wives who want their alimony, so shut the hell up and get in the car. I haven't got time to shoot the breeze with you. The boss is waiting. Move over, sweetheart. You're driving."

The man's gruff command drew Julie's attention and she glanced up at a point just beyond Dylan's shoulder. A steely black gaze fixed on her, and for the first time, she took a close look at the man who held the knife, rather than the actual weapon.

She'd seen him inside the restaurant with an extralarge malt in his hands and a camera strapped around his neck. He was in his midforties. Khaki shorts made his pale legs look even more stark. A Dallas Cowboys' T-shirt accentuated his potbelly and a faded ball cap perched on top of his head. He'd looked like yet another tourist who'd pulled in off the Interstate.

Except for the eyes. They revealed a coldness that told her he'd threatened a life many times before. Threatened, and worse.

"You deaf?" the man barked, and pressed the blade deeper into Dylan's neck. A small bead of red appeared and Julie's stomach somersaulted. "I said move over, or your loverboy here gets it good."

"I'm going," she said, her lips thick and her voice scratchy. "Just don't, okay? Please don't." She scrambled across the seat and slid behind the wheel. Dread churned her stomach and made her heart pound.

"Say, it seems like she's got a soft spot for you, buddy. Is that right, sweet cheeks? You got a soft spot for this guy?"

"He's my friend." As soon as the statement was out of her mouth, Julie saw Dylan tense. She didn't have time to wonder why. Instead, she kept looking around, searching for a way out. As her gaze lit on the car keys dangling from the ignition, a plan started to form.

"Friends, huh? Now ain't that sweet? I wish I had a friend as pretty as this one. She's a real looker. 'Course, I'd want her to be more than my friend. What do you say to that, sugar? You want to be more than friends with me?"

"Whatever you say."

"Hey, I like this girl. She's real cooperative. Just the way I like my women. And my men." He nudged Dylan. "Now get in real nice and slow and easy."

The minute Dylan bent to get into the car, his gaze caught Julie's. A warning flickered hot and bright, as if he read the thoughts racing through her mind. As if he wanted her to steer clear of them.

But she had to do something. One of the primary things she'd learned in all the self-defense classes she'd taken was to never let a stranger get close, much less into the confines of an automobile.

"So what happened to your kids?" Dylan asked in that same fearless monotone he'd used earlier, as if they were old friends making small talk.

As if he weren't this close to having his throat slit.

"They weren't mine," the man replied as he bent his knees to follow Dylan into the car. "Just a few loaners. Amazing what you can rent on the Internet these days...."

The next few moments passed in a frantic blur as Julie did the only thing she could. She turned the key in the ignition and shifted into reverse.

A loud squeal drowned out the man's vicious curse, the sudden move throwing his balance completely off. He slammed into Dylan's side for a frenzied moment before Dylan sprang into action, knocked the knife from the man's hands and shoved him out the swinging door.

"Go!" he ordered Julie as he grabbed the wayward door and hauled it closed.

Julie shifted into drive and slammed her foot

down on the gas pedal. The car sped forward, leaving the man sprawled in the dust behind them.

"Oh, God," Julie finally breathed as they turned onto the main road and left Billy Bob's behind. Her heart revved and she gasped for some fresh air that didn't taste of fear and dread. "That was close. He almost had—" Her words died as her gaze shifted to Dylan and she saw the trail of red oozing from his neck. "Ohmigod. He cut you."

"It's just a nick. Keep driving."

"But he *cut* you. He really cut you. We have to—"

"We will," he interrupted. "But for now we have to drive. We need to get back on the Interstate and farther down the road. Then we'll stop." He ripped open the glove box and retrieved the first-aid kit. Pulling out a roll of gauze, he tore a strip off, folded it and held it to the bleeding wound.

It wasn't until she felt the tear roll down her cheek that she realized she'd been crying. She wiped frantically at her face before glancing in the rearview mirror at her wailing child. Tears streaked his face and she knew he was scared.

"It's okay, baby," Julie soothed.

"That's right little man." Dylan leaned over the back seat and retrieved the baby's pacifier with his free hand. "You just settle down. Everything's all right."

"EVERYTHING IS all wrong," Julie told Dylan several hours later after he'd finally given the go-ahead and they'd pulled into a small convenience store, one of the last stops they'd made before they reached Bayou Blue, a small village situated about two hours away on the banks of one of Louisiana's most secluded swamps. Hattie lived just outside Bayou Blue, farther into the swamp.

So deep it was a wonder Sebastian had ever found her.

But he had.

Just as he'd found Julie.

"You knew he was close," Dylan told her as he unloaded the fresh bandages he'd just purchased inside the store. The neon sign flickered, casting a green glow across the front seat and the man seated just inches away. Thomas snored lightly from the car seat.

"He's always been close," Julie said, the day's events replaying in her head, stirring her fear. "But never right here."

"He isn't *here*." He pulled out a handful of cotton balls and soaked them with alcohol. "He's behind us again, and he'll stay that way as long as we don't slow down and we don't panic. That means we get to Hattie's place before them. We leave her place before them. We get the locket before them, and in the process, we get Sebastian before he gets us."

"And what if we can't get him? What if I'm wrong about the locket figuring into this somehow?"

"Then we go back into hiding before they find us again." When she started to protest, he added, "And we think of another way to get the upper hand with Sebastian so you and Thomas can stop hiding."

"You finally agree with me."

"Partly. I still think you should be hiding and I should do this myself."

"I'm doing this." Her gaze locked with his. "I need to do this. To do something. I've spent the past year letting the situation dictate to me. I can't do that anymore. I have to stand up for myself." She shook her head. "I know that's probably hard for you to understand. You're always in control of the situation instead of the other way around."

"Not always." He looked so defeated in that next instant that it touched something deep inside her. "I should have seen this guy coming tonight. I felt uneasy about him, but I thought it was the other guy I had to look out for because he was alone. He seemed suspicious. I shouldn't have let the kids throw me like that."

"There's no way you could have known it was a setup."

"It's my job."

"But this time it involves people you care about, which keeps you from thinking completely straight." Her fingertips trailed over his jaw. Stubble scratched across her skin as she traced the shape of his face, his chin.

It wasn't until she felt his fingers close around her wrist that she realized what she'd just done.

She'd touched him. Not the concerned touch of a caring friend, but the slow, soothing stroke of a woman who'd spent the past night dreaming of him.

"What are you doing?"

"I'm..." Her gaze fell on the blood-soaked bandage he held against his neck. "I'm trying to help you for a change." She shrugged free of his grip and took the alcohol-soaked cotton from his hand. "We need to get this wound cleaned and dressed."

She spent the next few minutes dabbing at his skin and trying to forget the man with the knife. But she was too skittish, the sight of Dylan's wound stirring her memory. Her fear.

"Talk to me," she finally blurted as she reached for some antibiotic cream.

"Why?"

She stared at the nasty cut and swallowed the lump in her throat. "I'm not too good with blood."

"I can clean it—" he started, but she slapped his hand away.

"It's the least I can do. You're always helping me. Always being such a good friend."

"That's me." He sounded irritated.

"Just talk to me. Tell me about Dallas." After college graduation, while she'd gone off to pursue a career in journalism, Dylan had entered the police academy. He'd spent several years with the San Antonio Police Department before moving to Dallas to do undercover work. "Why did you go?"

"I'd always wanted to get into undercover work, but San Antonio was too close to home. Dallas was a great opportunity."

"Weren't you lonely?"

"I was busy. Making detective was hard enough. Making lead detective was even harder."

"And?"

"And what?"

"Nothing else."

"You were there for five years. I'm sure you did more than work. Did you have friends?"

"Co-workers."

"How about girlfriends?" Now why had she asked that?

Because the old Julie would have asked. The Julie who'd always bugged him for help in her calculus class. The Julie who'd always been trying to set him up with one of her friends. Julie always wanted to know everything about his love life, or lack of, so she could help.

She told herself she was asking now for the same reason, but she knew in her heart there was more to it. The need to know went deeper.

"I dated a little. Not too much and never the same woman."

"Why not?"

"Because I never found the right woman."

Julie wasn't sure why she reached out to him in that next instant. Maybe it was the panic at

seeing the knife against his throat, the fear that
he would be hurt, that he would die, that finally
caught up to her. But suddenly, all the reasons
why she shouldn't feel attracted to Dylan Garrett faded. Liquid heat surged through her,
washing away her hesitation and her doubt, until she felt only a burning lust that demanded
instant satisfaction.

She leaned over and touched her lips to his.

She tasted his surprise for those first furious
heartbeats, before something much more basic
and elemental seemed to take over.

He groaned, the sound welling up from his
chest as his hands curved around her shoulders
and pulled her close. He returned her kiss, his
tongue and lips hot and urgent—as hot and urgent as her own.

Friends, a voice whispered someplace far, far
away, but the knowledge didn't scare her off.
It made the kiss even more intense because she
and Dylan already shared an emotional intimacy.

It was as if she'd unleashed something inside
him. Everything that followed seemed to move
at lightning speed as his hands slid down her
back to cup her buttocks. He urged one leg over

him until she sat straddling him, her back to the dash.

He pulled her close, cradling her hips against the rigid length of his erection, and awareness gripped every nerve. He wanted her just as much as she wanted him. The realization sent a wash of joy through her, followed by a fierce pang of doubt.

She wanted this closeness with him. She'd reached for him. She'd kissed him. But this was more than a kiss. Much more. Things were moving way too fast.

"No," she gasped as she wrenched her mouth free from his and pulled back enough to give herself some breathing room.

His eyes blinked open and she glimpsed the raw hunger in the blue depths. At least, she thought it was hunger. But then the fierce gleam faded into concern and she was left to wonder if she'd only imagined it.

Hoped for it.

Silence wrapped around them, the sound disrupted only by the frantic draw of air as they both fought for a calming breath.

"I'm sorry," she finally blurted, eager to dispel the awkward quiet. "I shouldn't have. I mean, we're friends."

"Friends don't kiss like that."

"That's my point. I didn't mean… It's just, I've been really uptight and I guess all the excitement from tonight finally got to me. I'm a little high-strung. I needed to work off some tension." It was a lame excuse, but it was all she could come up with to explain her actions. "I shouldn't have."

"No, *you* shouldn't have," he said.

She was right. She had stepped over the line and misjudged his response. It wasn't that he wanted *her*. He simply wanted. He'd been worked up, his adrenaline flowing from his brush with death. Of course he'd responded rather fiercely.

"*I* should have," he continued. "A long, long time ago."

And then Dylan Garrett did what she'd spent an entire sleepless night dreaming of—*he* kissed *her*.

CHAPTER SIX

HE'D KISSED HER.

The knowledge echoed through Julie's head as she watched him round the front of the car, open the driver's door and slide behind the wheel.

"Are you sure you can drive?"

"It's an automatic," he replied, shoving the keys into the ignition. "I'll be fine."

But would she? she wondered as he shifted into drive, arm flexing, muscles rippling. She shot a sideways glance at him, studying his profile as he steered the car out of the parking lot and onto the feeder road.

A few seconds later, they sped onto the Interstate for the last two-hour stretch until they reached the exit leading to Bayou Blue.

Images flitted through her mind—the knife-wielding man, the steely blade pressed to Dylan's throat. She blinked back the tears that suddenly burned her eyes.

She forced herself to focus on the passing road markers, counting down the exits until they finally swerved off the highway. A quick stop at a liquor store for some liquid painkiller for Dylan to take once they reached their destination, and then they were back on the road. A few more miles and they turned onto County Road 161.

Pasture lined the road for several miles before giving way to gigantic trees that crowded overhead. Spanish moss draped the lazy branches and fog clung to the ground, shrouding the path in a fuzzy gray.

"Are you sure this is the road?" he'd asked too many times to count.

"I know it's a little rough, but this is it." Julie would know this road anywhere. She'd traveled it many times going to and from town with various groceries for herself and the other women boarding at Hattie's.

But somehow driving along the familiar stretch felt different now. The tree-shrouded path had once seemed like salvation, the covering a godsend to a woman in hiding. Now it seemed eerie, threatening. She couldn't see beyond the trees to what might lie in wait just beyond them. But she could feel it. A strange dread prickled her nerve endings and sent unease crawling up and down her spine.

Couple that with the crazy whirlwind of emotion inside her and Julie Cooper was this close to having a full-blown anxiety attack.

He'd kissed *her.*

Her mind replayed the scene yet again. Dylan's lips touching hers. His arms pulling her close. His tongue plundering her mouth, stroking and coaxing and devouring. She'd felt his heart pounding in his chest.

Desire.

That's what she wanted to think. What her gut told her. But Julie knew better than to blindly trust her instincts. She'd let her feelings get in the way of the truth once before. She'd been so eager for a happily ever after that she'd completely ignored the warning signs that told her Sebastian wasn't the man for her. The man she'd thought him to be.

Not this time. She wasn't letting her wishful thinking mistake Dylan's eager kiss for true desire. He'd just had a near brush with death. He'd been anxious to feel alive. To feel, period. The kiss had been the best affirmation of his vitality.

Of her own, as well. She'd been frightened,

her heart pounding, her adrenaline rushing. The situation had undoubtedly contributed to her body's fierce reaction.

The heat of the moment.

Now that moment was over and it was back to reality.

She glanced behind her and checked on Thomas. As usual, the car ride had its lulling effect. He was dozing again, his head resting against the car seat, his lips clamped firmly around his pacifier.

He'd been through so much. He was such a good baby. He deserved so much more than a life on the run. He deserved calm. Peace. Happiness.

Everything she was going to give him, or die trying.

The notion sent a burst of fear through her, but she fought it back down, holding on to her determination the way she would a shield.

"Where are you going?" she asked when they reached the next county road. Instead of taking a left, as she'd instructed, he turned the opposite way, heading toward the small town of Blue Willow.

"Hattie obviously hid the locket well. If Sebastian's men couldn't find it, chances are it isn't going to be easy for us to find, either. Unless you know where it is?'' When she shook her head, he added, ''I bet you do.''

''She never told me.''

''Not verbally, but you know her habits, her quirks. You lived with her. If you think about it, you'll probably come up with a few places to start, and that's what we're doing. Giving you some time to think. And sleep. Besides, the last thing I want is another confrontation with one of Sebastian's men. When it's daylight I stand a better chance of seeing them coming.'' He cut a sideways glance at her. ''You were great this afternoon. Quick thinking.''

''My quick thinking nearly got you killed.'' She should have swerved in the opposite direction so that Dylan's assailant would have fallen away from the knife and Dylan's throat.

''I would have gotten far worse if that guy had climbed into the car with us and we'd taken off.''

''You think he would have harmed us?''

''Not you. They need you to find the locket since they're not having much luck on their own. You would have been safe.''

''And what about you?''

"I'm a nuisance. A pest. I'm better off out of the way."

Her gaze rested again on the bandage at his neck. A red stain had seeped through. "Oh, God, I'm so sorry, Dylan. I almost got you killed."

"For you and Thomas? I consider it a worthy cause."

The words didn't make her feel any better, but she tried to believe them anyway. The last thing she needed right now was guilt. Or fear. Or panic. She needed to stay calm. To relax and think. Otherwise, she would never find the locket.

And he was right about one thing. Thomas was a worthy cause. He was a small child who deserved a normal life, and Julie was going to give it to him.

"So who was the other guy? The one that Sebastian's man mentioned?"

"I had a little encounter in the men's room. I thought the guy was after us, too, but I was wrong."

"So who did he work for?"

"I'm still trying to figure that out, though I have a pretty good idea."

They fell into a companionable silence then and Julie settled into the seat.

The locket.

She let her mind drift back to the days she'd spent at Hattie's place. She remembered Hattie showing her the old navy trunk—a relic from her marriage to her first husband back in the fifties—that she kept hidden beneath a board in the floor of her bedroom. Then there'd been the scarred flour jar containing the wad of bills she'd tucked away in the back of the pantry. All possibilities.

She leaned her head back against the leather headrest and forced all thoughts from her mind. The steady hum of the engine sent a laziness creeping through her until her eyes drifted shut.

With the vents blowing cool air and Dylan's body a handspan away from her, the soft seat lulling her muscles and turning them to marshmallows, she had the odd thought that she never wanted to be anyplace else. She felt safe and protected and, for once in her life, not so lonely.

For a brief moment, she let herself forget about the past year and pretend that she was meant to be here in this car, next to this man, and in much more than a friendly capacity. He was hers and she was his and...

Thankfully, she drifted into unconsciousness before she could finish the thoughts. But her dreams took over from there, and what Julie's conscience had hesitated to complete, her subconscious took great pleasure in seeing through to the very end.

HE WAS DEFINITELY going to make her pay.

Sebastian listened to Cap Pendleton, a crack shot and one of the best hired guns in the business, recount the day's events over the phone. His temper burned hotter with each word.

"She practically ran me over," Cap growled. "Jeez, I've got bruises and a scraped knee and I busted out a tooth when I hit the ground."

Sebastian gritted his teeth and snapped. "So you let her go? Is that what you're saying?"

"Did you hear me? She nearly killed me!"

"I'll kill you if you don't get back on her tail. She's obviously headed to Devereaux's place. The locket *is* there."

"I don't give a crap about your locket. What about my tooth? What are you going to do—"

"Shut up," Sebastian seethed. "If you'd done the job right, you wouldn't be such a mess. You can forget about a bonus—come to think of it, I'm not even sure I should pay you at all.''

''What do you mean?''

''You heard what I said.'' Sebastian slammed down the phone. He didn't normally do any kind of grunt work. He'd worked hard not to have to dirty his hands with such petty stuff, but obviously Pendleton wasn't up to the job.

This was important. He'd have to go out to the Devereaux place himself.

Only once before had he stooped to such menial work. But he'd had to prove himself, and so he'd actually kidnapped a woman to show Crowe that he was a loyal and worthy business partner.

The crime boss had been convinced and had given Sebastian a nice chunk of the change coming through courtesy of various illegal venues. Drugs. Gambling. Money laundering.

Crowe controlled it all.

Controlled as in past tense. The man was in prison now, using Silva to run things on the outside. Silva wasn't nearly the generous sort his boss was. He didn't like Sebastian.

And Sebastian didn't like him, nor did he like taking orders from him and catering to him.

Not for long. The locket would solve all his problems, which meant the piece of jewelry was far too important to trust with anyone but himself.

He intended to be there when Julie retrieved it.

And then he would silence her for good.

"WAKE UP, sleepyhead."

Julie opened her eyes and stared up at Dylan, who leaned into the open passenger door, his face inches from hers, breath warm on her skin.

She blinked, feeling the heat and her own exhaustion.

"Are we there already?" she grumbled, closing her eyes again. She would rather go back to the dream she'd been having. To the cool, crisp sheets and the warm man...

"Come on," he said. Had her head not felt so heavy, she might have opened her eyes again. Instead, she turned, nuzzling the warm leather headrest.

"I'll just stay here," she murmured.

"No chance, Sleeping Beauty," he said, his voice deep, husky and so very close to her ear. She felt his arms under her legs, around her back. Then he hoisted her from the front seat and pulled her out into the humid night. His heated curse blistered her ears and the last remnants of the dream faded. He was in pain.

Her eyes snapped open. "What are you doing? Put me down. You're going to open up your wound again."

"I'm fine. I'm not going to let you down now that you've put me to all this trouble." His face was set in a grimace, his mouth a hard line. "Just relax." He turned and headed for the shabby-looking motel that loomed about twenty feet in front of them. A porch spanned the perimeter and a flashing neon sign proudly announced Last Stop Inn.

"You don't have to do this. I can walk," she insisted. She caught a glimpse over his shoulder at the open car door and her heart did a dangerous flip.

As if Dylan read her thoughts, he said, "Thomas is already sound asleep inside. I took care of him first, and now I'm taking care of you."

As usual.

She went still, noticing the tightness around his mouth, the slightly glazed look in his eyes. The curse he'd muttered when he'd pulled her from the car rang in her ears. It must be killing him to carry her like this, but still, he didn't put her down.

At last they reached the room and Dylan deposited her on the bed. She swayed from fatigue and he caught her easily with his good arm.

"In bed," he told her, yanking back the sheets on the double bed and steering her down to the edge. "We've got a few hours until daybreak and I want you rested."

"What about you?"

"Don't worry about me."

She eyed him, stiffening as she met his gaze. "It works both ways, you know. You worry about me, so I can worry about you." She reached up and touched his shoulder. "We should change those bandages."

"Later. I'm going to the laundry room. The clerk said we have to get our own clean sheets and towels because the maid was out sick today, and since this place is so small, there was no replacement for her."

"He couldn't fold towels himself?"

"There's an LSU game on. He was glued to the TV set. I'll be back."

Dylan disappeared and Julie found herself alone in the motel room with a sleeping Thomas, who snored soundly in the portable crib Dylan must have got from the clerk. She ran a hand over the fluffy pillow. As inviting as it was, the doorway off to one side of the room called her name even louder.

A few minutes later, she flicked on the bathroom light, opened the shower doors and switched the warm water on. She thought briefly about her lack of towels, then opted to put her clothes back on wet if Dylan didn't return on time. She pulled off her T-shirt and pushed down her jeans. Minutes later, she stepped beneath the warm spray.

Heaven. She'd found pure heaven.

Julie relished the temporary reprieve and let her questions slip away along with the tension that held her muscles tight. She didn't think of Sebastian or the man who'd knifed Dylan or anything save one very sexy dream man.

CHAPTER SEVEN

DYLAN DIDN'T mean to look. Under normal circumstances, he wouldn't have. No use looking at what you couldn't have. But things had changed over the past twenty-four hours. He was through denying himself, and he was through letting her deny him.

When she pushed open the shower door and one slender arm shot out to grope for a towel, his groin tightened.

When she discovered the rack was still empty, the shapely silhouette behind the glass stepped into full view, and a flame lit in Dylan's belly.

His grip tightened on the towel in his hands. Her towel. All he'd meant to do was bring in one of the clean linens he'd picked up in the registration office, along with an ice bucket and a coupon for a free stack of pancakes at Dotties—the café just across the street.

He should leave. He knew that. He'd had

every intention of draping the towel on the rack while she finished her shower. In and out, without her being the wiser. Now was not the time for a confrontation. The kiss had been enough progress for tonight.

As well as an eye-opening experience.

He had to go slow with her. He hadn't made love to a woman in over a year and a half, since her disappearance. He'd faced his feelings for Julie then and realized that he would never, ever find a woman to take her place. He didn't want to find one. He'd only wanted her.

Then and now.

One touch of her lips and he'd lost control. He didn't want to do that. He couldn't afford to scare her off when she just seemed to be coming around.

She'd felt the desire. The heat.

Slow. That's what he told himself. He was going to take things slow and easy.

If only his body would go along with the plan. Instead, his blood raced ninety miles to nothing through his system. And there was nothing easy about the hard response of his body at the sight of her.

Water beaded across her creamy skin, slid seductively down to drip on the carpet. She passed her hands over her face and through her wet hair before opening her eyes.

A dozen emotions flashed across her face. Surprise, anger, fear and something else. The very same emotion that blazed across his nerve endings and made him keep looking when he knew he should turn away.

Hunger.

He recognized it, and his erection grew even harder.

She might have thought their kiss a mistake. Maybe she still did, but at that moment, more than anything, she wanted a taste of him. He saw it in her sudden swallow, the way her lips parted and her tongue darted out to sweep across the fullness of her bottom lip.

"What are you doing in here?" The words came out on a rush of breath, and her breasts quivered with the effort. Dylan's gaze dropped, devoured the full, rounded globes tipped with cinnamon-colored nipples that pebbled at a glance and seemed to beg his attention.

Attention he gladly gave. He couldn't help himself. He'd spent a lifetime waiting for this woman.

He caressed her with his eyes, wishing like anything it was his tongue circling the distended tips, gathering the drops of water from the puckered flesh. He wanted a taste of her more than he'd ever wanted anything before.

He took a step inside the bathroom, his feet moving almost of their own volition. What was he doing? He should toss her the towel, turn and walk out. He would have, if she hadn't been staring at him with those wide, hungry eyes—eyes that called him forward even as common sense pulled him back.

Yes, he should leave.

He didn't.

"I..." She caught her bottom lip between her teeth as if she'd run out of words. She, who could talk up a storm when the notion hit her. She'd talked his ear off on more than one occasion, confided in him, trusted him.

Friends.

The notion sent a burst of determination through him and he took another step toward her.

"You," he murmured, his voice raw, echoing the strange ache gripping his body, "are all wet." Another step and his body blazed hotter, his gaze lingering on her mouth. The most kissable mouth he'd ever seen.

She turned a deep shade of crimson, as if

realizing her naked state. Dylan had the incredible urge to reach out, pull her into his arms and shield her, but he didn't.

Instead, he let his gaze sweep the length of her, lingering on the inviting patch of gold curls at the apex of her thighs. His smile faltered and a shudder went through him.

She was beautiful, and she was right here. An arm's length away. And she wanted him. He saw the desire hot in her gaze, even brighter than when she'd kissed him earlier that evening.

She'd kissed *him,* and not some friendly peck on the cheek. If he'd had any doubts about Julie seeing him as a man, they'd been extinguished the minute she'd pressed her lips to his, as if she couldn't quite believe he was alive and at her fingertips.

As if she feared he might disappear and she might lose that one moment forever.

But Dylan had no intention of disappearing. He was here and he was staying here, and they had plenty of time. He didn't want to screw this up by rushing into something she still might not be ready for. He wouldn't push her, and so he tossed her the towel.

The action gave him one last glimpse of those perfect, cinnamon-tipped breasts as she moved to catch it. Then he turned and retreated into the bedroom, closing the bathroom door behind him.

Slow.

He drew in a deep breath and fought to calm down his body. Checking on Thomas, who slept soundly in his portable crib, Dylan ran a finger over the child's chubby cheek and smiled. Then he walked over to the dresser, retrieved the small bottle of whiskey he'd picked up at the liquor store and made his way back to the bed. Sinking down on the edge, he fixed his gaze on the bathroom door.

Minutes passed. He heard her moving around, but still the door didn't open. He unscrewed the cap on the bottle and downed a huge swallow, grimacing at the heat that scorched his throat.

By the time he took the next swig, the liquid had lost its bite. He drank another swallow, wishing like anything he had a bottle of painkillers. It was just a flesh wound, but it was deep. He didn't normally drink. Not like this. But a liquor store had been easier to find than a pharmacy, and there'd be neither in this town. No fast-food restaurants, or pizza parlors. No

round-the-clock convenience store. Nothing
that stayed open past five in the afternoon.

The whiskey would do the trick. Help him
sleep a little and maybe forget the woman in
the bathroom. Yes, it was better if he simply
put her out of his mind for now.

Two more swallows and he stretched back
out on the bed, not bothering to climb beneath
the covers. While he'd taken every precaution
to make sure that no one had followed them—
he'd backtracked on the highway twice before
circling back around and exiting for the country
road that had led here.

No one had followed. He felt it deep in his
bones, his gut. A calm that seeped through and
lulled his eyes shut when he normally would
have been wired. He, Julie and Thomas were
safe. For now.

But tomorrow…

They would be at Hattie's, and Dylan would
be prepared for whatever happened.

He closed his eyes. Through a sleepy fog, he
heard the door opening. Soft footsteps padded
across the floor. He willed his eyes to open,
wanting one more glimpse of her before he
gave in to the exhaustion tugging at his muscles, but the effort was too much. He was so

tired, his head heavy, and it was all he could do just to keep his ears alert. The sounds came from far away…the soft rustle of fabric, then the creak of floorboards.

He waited to hear the squeaking of bed-springs or the whisper of sheets, but she must have decided to keep her distance.

The knowledge sang through his head, filling him with a rush of satisfaction. Maybe he had, indeed, succeeded in getting Julie to see him as more than a best buddy.

He wanted to open his eyes, to catch one more glimpse of her to fuel his dreams before he gave in to the warmth seeping through him. Not that he had to. She was there in his sub-conscious—creamy, satiny skin, cinnamon-tipped nipples that throbbed and puckered at the flick of his tongue, and the softest, most yield-ing mouth he'd ever tasted. She hovered over him, a sultry smile on her face as she reached out.

"Dylan?" He heard the soft murmur of his name. It might have been his imagination, but he could have sworn he heard the desperation and frustration that he himself was feeling in that one word. It was a question, an invitation, a plea…a very real plea that echoed in his head.

And the dream that followed seemed just as real, and very pleasant. Nothing like the violent dreams he'd grown accustomed to after years with the Dallas PD. Instead, he felt her hands, the brush of her skin, her warmth…

In fact, he could almost believe it wasn't a dream at all, but real. As real as the pulsing length of his erection, which begged for satisfaction. For her.

Then again, if it had been real, he wouldn't have allowed himself to touch her. Not yet. He was trying to give her some time to come to terms with her newfound awareness of him.

But in his dream he touched her freely, boldly, leaving not an inch of her unexplored. He sank inside her, felt her tighten around him, draw him deeper.

In his dream Julie became one with him.

The trouble was, a dream wasn't enough. Dylan wanted more.

THE SOFT CRY pushed past the sleepy fog holding Dylan hostage and his eyes snapped open. He blinked several times before his vision focused on the numbers glaring in red neon from the bedside table. He felt as if he'd been sleeping forever when, in reality, it was just two hours later.

Another cry and his gaze shifted to the baby lying on his back in his bed next to Dylan. Thomas waved a fist before putting his fingers in his mouth and sucking.

A soft sigh drifted across the room and Dylan turned to see the woman curled up in the chair, the nightstand lamp bathing her in a pale-yellow glow that made her complexion look warmer, more golden than he remembered. With her arms wrapped about her, feet tucked up beneath the edges of an oversize T-shirt, she looked so small. So fragile.

She wasn't. She was a strong woman. She'd lived on the run—alone and pregnant, then with a small child—and she'd survived.

Admiration welled inside him, along with the need to hold her, touch her, kiss her...*slow*.

Another cry and his attention shifted back to Thomas.

"You hungry, little fella?"

The baby waved his fist wildly and gurgled and Dylan smiled. Thomas had Sebastian's dark hair, but that's where the resemblance ended. His eyes were wide and bright blue and warm—

just like his mother's. And when he smiled he had the faintest dimples, just like Julie.

"Come on, fella," Dylan said as he gathered the baby close and reached over for the clean bottle and can of formula on the bedside table. Quickly he opened the can and filled the bottle. At least it would be room temperature. Cradling the baby in his arms, he settled back against the headboard, knees bent, feet flat on the bed, and slid the nipple into Thomas's eager mouth.

The baby sucked wildly, waving his fists a few minutes more before settling into Dylan's arms.

Dylan had always liked children. His partner for five years back in Dallas had had four of them, and Dylan had spent many Sundays at Dave's house. Wrestling with his eight-year-old. Tickling his five-year-old. Reading stories to the three-year-old. Rocking the six-month-old. But he'd never felt the warmth that filled him at this moment.

There was just something about the way Thomas clung to one of Dylan's fingers, his other chubby fist tucked beneath his chin as he sucked his bottle. Slowly, his eyes drifted shut once again.

"He likes you."

Julie's voice drew his attention and Dylan lifted his head to find her watching him.

"Of course he does." He winked and fingered the bottle. "I've got the goods."

"No, he really likes you. He doesn't let just anyone hold him." She cleared her throat, as if the thought had stirred a lump. "He used to let Hattie hold him." She swallowed again and licked her lips. "He's comfortable with you," she finally said.

"He's a great kid. You're lucky."

"I am." A light shone in her eyes. "In more ways than one." The room was quiet, the only sound that of cold air rushing from the air conditioner. "You're a good friend to me, Dylan. I'm so sorry you were hurt tonight."

Friend. The word echoed through his head, stirring his irritation.

"We've already been over that. It's nothing." He settled a soundly sleeping Thomas in his crib and tucked a blanket around him before swinging his legs over the side of the bed. His gaze locked with Julie's. "I don't want your gratitude, Julie. That's the last thing I want." He stood and took a step toward her. "I want more from you than that."

"Don't." She shook her head. "I know what you're going to say."

Another step. "I want you."

"You don't." She shook her head and turned toward the window. "I mean, you do, but it's only because I'm a woman. I could be any woman, and you could be any man."

"Is that what you really think?"

He watched the indecision play across her face before she nodded. "It's true."

He felt a surge of anger because he didn't want to be *any* man to Julie. He wanted to be her man.

"So any woman would make me this hard?" His question drew her attention and she lowered her gaze, obviously noting the bulge of his erection.

Something flickered in her gaze and she swallowed before managing a nod. "I—I guess so."

He reached out then, trailing his fingers down her collarbone, over the soft cotton of her T-shirt to where her nipples formed tight little buds beneath the material. Her breath caught, but she didn't shrink away from him, and Dylan knew that, as surprised as she was, she was just as excited.

He *knew* it, but he wanted her to admit it.

"And any man would make your nipples this hard?" He fingered one ripe tip.

"Y-yes," she managed on a sharp intake of breath.

"And what about goose bumps?" He touched her shoulder, trailed his fingers down her arm until flesh met flesh and her skin prickled. "Would any man do this to you?"

"I, um," she licked her lips. "I—I think so."

"And what about the heat, darlin'?" His fingertip dipped below the hem of her T-shirt and touched the triangle of satin. She drew in a sharp breath, her gaze never wavering from his. "Would any man make you this hot?" He dipped past the elastic of her panties and touched the slick folds between her legs. "This wet?"

"I..." She struggled for a breath. "I—I don't know."

"Then let's see what we can do about making up your mind."

CHAPTER EIGHT

SHE SHOULD STOP. She *needed* to stop.

She wasn't going to stop.

Julie admitted that to herself as Dylan slanted his head and deepened the kiss she hadn't been able to resist. His tongue plunged into her mouth to tangle with hers and she forgot every reason why she shouldn't be here like this with this man.

When he kissed just so, it seemed too right. As if they were meant to be together like this but had simply failed to find their way until now. Dylan made everything else fade into the background until she saw only him, smelled only him, felt only him.

And he felt right.

Her hand went to his chest and she felt his heartbeat. The drumming matched hers as their tongues battled first, then probed, then tasted the other in a kiss unlike any she had ever experienced.

It was fast and furious and she found herself pulling away, gasping for air.

"I..." she began.

"I want this, but only if you're sure," he said, mistaking her hesitation for doubt. "Only if you want me. *Me*."

She touched his jaw, rough and shadowed with stubble. Slowly, she moved her fingers down the taut muscles of his neck, then lower, over the hard chest muscles to the satiny ripples of his stomach.

Dylan stood still beneath her probing, his body rigid.

When she moved to dip her hands beneath the waist of his jeans, he caught her wrists. "I'm not just any man," he said, his voice rough, raw with the desire sparking in the blue depths of his eyes. "And you're not just any woman. You do this to me." He touched her fingers to the hard length beneath the zipper of his jeans. *"You."* He urged one of her hands down between her own thighs. "And I do this to you."

Julie felt the heat through her pants, scorching her palm. The touch sent need spiraling through her.

He released her, then waited, his muscles still taut.

This time when her fingers went to the waist-band of his jeans, he didn't stop her. She heard his sharp intake of breath as she undid the button and slid the zipper down. She let her fingers linger at his erection, which throbbed and grew beneath her attention. Then she felt her way up his stomach, around his waist. She moved her hands up his back, over his shoulder blades, feeling the smooth, fiery skin beneath her fingertips and marveling at the raw power of flesh and blood.

"Julie," he groaned, still not touching her, still not relaxing beneath her exploration. "I hope you know what you're doing. Because once you start this, you can't stop. I won't let you," he said, his voice tight, almost pained. "I can't. I've wanted it too long."

"So have I," she whispered. "So have I."

With a throaty growl, Dylan locked his arms around her and pulled her closer. He touched his lips to hers none too gently, sucking the breath from her body with his hungry mouth. She returned his fervor, losing herself in the storm of feeling that rose inside of her.

When Dylan eased her legs up on either side

of him and lifted her, she wrapped her arms about his neck. A moment later, he pressed her back against the bed, then leaned away.

"Julie."

At the sound of her name, she opened her eyes and stared up into the stormy depths of his.

"Don't close your eyes. I want to see everything that you feel. Every emotion when I touch you." He fingered the edges of her T-shirt.

With the expertise of a man well skilled in the art of lovemaking, he eased the shirt over her head and then trailed his hands down the creamy skin of her arms. "How does it feel when I touch you here?" With one finger he traced the outline of first one nipple, then the next. "Answer me," he demanded in a soft voice. "How does it feel?"

"Like you're touching me—*you*." She murmured the only word that came to mind.

He smiled, then dipped his head to close his mouth over one swollen nipple. Julie gasped and wound her fingers in the silky roughness of his hair.

He sucked and nuzzled the throbbing tip until Julie cried out. Then he kissed his way to the other, to inflict the same delicious torture. And his mouth was as warm as his body...and as real.

Her nerves were alive as he moved his hands down to her waist. He leaned away from her then, letting the air breeze over her heated skin.

"You closed your eyes," he said.

Guilty, Julie lifted her heavy lids to stare up at him through a veil of lashes.

"That's better." Their gazes locked as he slid her panties off in one sweeping motion.

When he stood, Julie leaned up on her elbows, intrigued by the lean lines of his body. He was perfection, she thought as he slid his jeans down over his hips, down his muscled thighs. His erection stood proud in the lamplight and she swallowed, afraid, yet thrilled at the same time.

Maneuvering himself down beside her, he pressed his hardness against her thigh. Then, with slow exploration, he moved his hand across her abdomen, down to the triangle of hair.

He kissed her cheek as he cupped the heated flesh between her legs. "So wet," he said, slipping one finger inside the soft folds. Julie arched her back, pushing herself into his palm, drawing his finger deeper.

"You like that?"

She nodded, staring up at him, her lips parted, her body craving more.

"And this?" He slipped another finger inside and Julie felt the tense coil in her stomach wind dangerously tighter.

She took a ragged breath, then another and another as Dylan played inside her, driving her toward the edge of reality, into the world beyond—filled with excruciating pleasure and sweet, sweet pain.

Gasping, she arched her hips for him. Deeper, deeper his fingers pushed, caressing, stroking until her legs trembled violently and her mind reeled from the sensations flooding through her. Then he eased his hand away.

"Dylan?" She forced her eyes open, to find him studying her heated face.

"It's okay," he murmured. He grabbed her wrist and pressed a lingering kiss to her palm. "I feel you, Julie—your wanting, your need. Can you feel it?" He guided her hand over her cheek, down the column of her throat.

Her skin, hot beneath her fingers, trembled from the touch—*her* touch. Dylan continued to guide her along. When she touched one nipple, the peak rose even higher. She tried to pull away, frightened by her reaction, but Dylan held her steady.

"Don't," he said. "Feel yourself, Julie. Feel what I feel." He swept her hand down across her stomach to the pulsing center of her body.

With his hand over hers, they stroked the damp flesh between her legs until Julie writhed and whimpered, desperate for release.

Dylan made her an active participant in his game of torture, as well as his willing victim, and she reveled in every nerve-wrenching sensation. More, she wanted more. More of him, more of herself.

She cried out, feeling the slippery wetness on her fingers. She bucked against the invasion as release jolted through her. Dylan held her hand steady, making sure she felt every quiver as she spiraled higher.

"You're so beautiful," he whispered, his lips a steady vibration at her temple. He let go of her hand to feel his way up the length of her body, to filter his fingers through her hair. "I've wanted you for so long."

She could feel him, hard, hot against her thigh, and was aware of a renewed tightening inside. Perspiration trickled between her

GET 2

HOW TO GET YOUR
2 FREE BOOKS AND FREE GIFT!

1. Peel off the MIRA sticker on the front cover. Place it in the space provided at right. This automatically entitles you to receive two free books and an exciting surprise gift.

2. Send back this card and you'll get 2 "The Best of the Best™" novels. The books have a combined cover price of $11.98 or more in the U.S. and $13.98 or more in Canada, but they are yours to keep absolutely FREE!

3. There's <u>no</u> catch. You're under <u>no</u> obligation to buy anything. We charge nothing – ZERO – for your first shipment. And you don't have to make an minimum number of purchases – not even one!

4. We call this line "The Best of the Best" because each month you'll receive the best books by some of today's most popular authors. These authors show up time and time again on all the major bestseller lists and their books sell out as soon as they hit the stores. You'll like the convenience of getting them delivered to your home at our special discount prices . . . and you'll love your *Heart to Heart* subscriber newsletter featuring author news, horoscopes, recipes, book reviews and much more!

SPECIAL FREE GIFT!

We'll send you a fabulous surprise gift, absolutely FREE, simply for accepting our no-risk offer!

5. We hope that after receiving your free books you'll want to remain a subscriber. But the choice is yours – to continue or cancel, anytime at all! So why not take us up on our invitation, with no risk of any kind. You'll be glad you did!

6. And remember...we'll send you a surprise gift ABSOLUTELY FREE just for giving "The Best of the Best" a try.

Visit us online at
www.mirabooks.com

® and TM are trademarks of Harlequin Enterprises Limited.

BOOKS FREE!

The Best of the Best™ — Here's How it Works:

Accepting your 2 free books and gift places you under no obligation to buy anything. You may keep the books and gift and return the shipping statement marked "cancel." If you do not cancel, about a month later we will send you 4 additional novels and bill you just $4.49 each in the U.S., or $4.99 each in Canada, plus 25¢ shipping & handling per book and applicable taxes if any.* That's the complete price and — compared to cover prices of $5.99 or more each in the U.S. and $6.99 or more each in Canada — it's quite a bargain! You may cancel at any time, but if you choose to continue, every month we'll send you 4 more books, which you may either purchase at the discount price or return to us and cancel your subscription.

*Terms and prices subject to change without notice. Sales tax applicable in N.Y. Canadian residents will be charged applicable provincial taxes and GST.

BUSINESS REPLY MAIL
FIRST-CLASS MAIL   PERMIT NO. 717-003   BUFFALO, NY

POSTAGE WILL BE PAID BY ADDRESSEE

THE BEST OF THE BEST
3010 WALDEN AVE
PO BOX 1867
BUFFALO NY 14240-9952

NO POSTAGE
NECESSARY
IF MAILED
IN THE
UNITED STATES

breasts. He dipped his head and licked a drop, sending a shiver through her body.

Before she could think of a reply, he reached down and pulled a foil packet from the pocket of his discarded jeans.

Julie watched, her mouth dry, as he ripped open the packet and began to stretch the contents over his rock-hard length. Driven by her need for him, and a newfound sense of freedom, she touched his hands. She forced his fingers away, then eased hers around the smooth, pulsing shaft, feeling it swell beneath her fingertips.

Dylan groaned, letting Julie slip the second skin the rest of the way down.

"How does that feel?" She lingered at the base of his manhood to stroke the smooth flesh.

"Not half as good as you're going to feel." He grabbed her by the hips and positioned her legs on either side of him. He pulled her down, driving into her until no space separated them.

He filled her, completely, perfectly, and Julie bit her lip to stifle the cry that sprang from her throat.

She grasped his shoulders, digging her nails into the hard muscled flesh as he gripped her bottom. He moved her up, then down the length of him. The motion, slow, steady at first, stoked the already blazing fire between her legs.

White-hot flame shot through her body and soon she moved of her own accord.

"You're so warm, so wet," he murmured, kissing the base of her throat.

His words pushed her even further than his feverish hands. She rose for the last time. With a shuddering cry, she slid down, drawing him fully inside. The room around her disintegrated, the floor fell away and tears slipped down her cheeks.

She wasn't prepared for her reaction. For the warmth that spread through her, the burst of tenderness.

This was rough and raw and physical. *Any* man.

That's what she wanted to think, but Julie had the hunch that no matter how far she searched or how long, she would never find a man like Dylan Garrett.

She ignored the disturbing thought. She wasn't going to worry over the future with all its danger and complications. She would face tomorrow when it came, along with the inevitable regrets and the knowledge that she'd lost her best friend in the entire world for a night of pleasure.

But now... Now was all about Dylan and the way it felt to be in his arms. And the pleasure...

Mmm, yes...tonight was all about pleasure.

DYLAN THROBBED inside her, exploding with earthshaking intensity as her muscles clenched him. She filled his senses—the scent of her, the feel of her, the sight of her lost in the throes of an orgasm.

He slid his hands up her sweat-soaked back, to weave his fingers into her damp hair. Burying his face in the soft swell of her breasts, he held her close. He felt every quiver of her body, every erratic breath, the pounding of her heart as it beat a rapid tattoo against his own.

Finally, he leaned away from her and stared into her face—at her parted lips still swollen from his kisses, her closed eyes framed with a long sweep of golden lashes, the wetness glistening on her cheeks. With gentle fingers, he wiped the tears away.

"What's wrong?"

At the sound of his voice, she opened her eyes. He saw a multitude of emotions reflected there—confusion, bewilderment, and ultimately, satisfaction.

"No one's ever made you feel the way that I did."

"Humble, aren't you?" she asked.

"Actually, darlin', the sight of you is pretty darned humbling." His gaze traveled over the smooth column of her neck, the delicate curve of her shoulders, to her full breasts, which rose and fell in a steady rhythm that stirred his blood.

No morning sunrise or starlit night could match the beauty of her skin, still damp and flushed from their lovemaking. And at that moment, Dylan felt more humble than he ever had before.

Then again, he'd known it. He'd known she would be different. Special. He'd slept with numerous women, searching for someone to make him forget her deep-blue eyes and her sweet smile. Someone to make his heart pound faster at just a glance. Someone to make him hot and hard at nothing more than the sight of her curvy body.

No one had ever come close.

He let his fingers drift down the curve of her

jaw, memorizing every line as if he couldn't quite believe she was real. And his.

For the moment.

Dylan pushed aside the thought and focused on the here and now, on the steady beat of her heart and the sweet scent of her skin and the fact that he wasn't going to let her go. She was his. Now and forever.

She just didn't know it yet.

"Answer my question," he demanded, his voice quiet, compelling. "When's the last time a man made you feel the way I just did."

"No," she challenged, her eyes sparkling with mischief. "I don't kiss and tell."

He grasped her hips and pressed her back onto the bed. The swift motion pushed him a fraction deeper into her moist heat and they both trembled.

"I didn't ask you about kissing," he murmured when he could breath again. "That was your first orgasm."

"No," she breathed, her eyes hooded, her features mirroring the ecstasy his touch brought her. "My second."

It was Dylan's turn to smile. "But you had a hand in the first one, sweetheart. I want to know if anyone has ever made you feel the way

I did the *second* time." He traced the pout of her bottom lip with his tongue. "Have you ever felt the hunger driving you on, demanding to be satisfied...then the explosion...like the world stops rotating for those few seconds and nothing else seems to matter?"

"No," The one word was a breathless whisper. "Not like that. Never that intense."

He smiled, the knowledge singing through his head, firing his blood all over again. He licked a drop of perspiration that trailed down the valley between her breasts. She trembled, then gasped as he outlined one aching nipple with his tongue.

He eased his hands beneath her bottom and cupped her buttocks. In response, she moaned, wiggling her hips and drawing him deeper.

After what had just happened, he should have been prepared for the fire that ignited between them.

He wasn't. Over the next hour, it was as if he hadn't touched her, stroked her, loved her. The feelings were just as wondrous, as intense as the first time, and Dylan found himself wondering how in the world he would ever be able to let her go.

And he would have to. Sebastian wasn't sim-

ply going to disappear. He was going to make
things as difficult as possible.

As deadly.

Doubts rushed through him, along with a
deep-seated dread for what awaited them tomorrow. But for the first time, Dylan ignored
his instinct and focused on the positive. On the
satiny feel of her skin and the deep, even sound
of her breathing and the freshness of her hair.

He refused to think beyond this moment.
He'd waited too long for this and he intended
to relish every second. As much as he hated to
admit it, he had the gut feeling that it would be
over all too quickly.

And damned if he didn't know only too well
that his instinct rarely steered him wrong.

CHAPTER NINE

THEY'D MADE LOVE.

Not love, Julie reminded herself as she sat on the edge of the bed just before daybreak the next morning and watched Dylan pull on his T-shirt. *Lust.*

He was wearing faded jeans that hugged his thighs to perfection and a soft cotton T-shirt. For a fleeting moment, she had a vision of him as he'd been the night before, dark and naked and powerful as he'd pressed her into the mattress and made love to her.

Not love. *Lust.*

Last night had been purely physical. She didn't love Dylan, nor did he love her.

Sure, she felt for him. They were good friends and it was only natural that she would feel such tenderness when she looked at him. But love?

Julie didn't trust herself when it came to that emotion. Never again.

"Penny for your thoughts," he said as he pulled her to her feet and stared down at her. "Then again, maybe I'd rather not know." For a split second, he actually looked worried, but the expression faded.

"Come on," he persisted. "What are you thinking?"

That I liked last night. That I want another night just like it. And another. And—

"That we'd better hit the road if we want to get an early start."

Never again.

They were friends, first and foremost.

But as Julie stared up at Dylan, the last thing she felt was friendly toward him. The realization sent a rush of sadness through her. She'd known it would happen. Last night had forever changed their relationship. There would be no going back. No companionable evenings spent watching the Spurs on TV. No shared pizzas. Never again would she be able to look at him and not think about what they'd done.

Her eyes blurred.

"You're having regrets?" His deep voice echoed in her ears.

She sniffled and wiped at her eyes. "It's just...we're friends. We were friends."

"We're still friends."

"No, not after last night. We can't take it back."

"No matter how much you want to?"

Did she feel regret?

Yes. No. Maybe. That was the trouble. She didn't know. Her instincts told her one thing, but she'd learned the hard way never to trust those instincts.

"I'm sorry."

"It's not your fault."

"I lost control. I—I was still so worked up over what happened and then I saw you and...I'm really sorry."

"I'm not. I don't regret last night. Not one minute. I needed last night, and so did you."

Need, as in the need to feel alive and forget that death was dogging them at every step. That was the truth, yet when he stared at her as he was doing right now, she could almost believe he was talking about a different sort of need. The kind that meant happily ever after.

If Julie had been a betting woman, she would have put her money on the fact that he actually felt something for her. Something deep and pure and strong enough to make her heart skip its next beat.

But she wasn't a betting woman. She'd lost too much already on what she'd thought to be a sure thing.

Never again.

"It shouldn't have happened." She shook her head. "Because of it, things will never be the same between us."

"That's what I'm counting on, darlin'. That's what I'm counting on."

LORD, he wanted to hold her.

He watched from the corner of his eye as she sat in the passenger seat, her hands clasped in her lap as they drove the final distance down the winding dirt road that led to Hattie's place.

She was thinking about the old woman. He could tell from her expression that the drive was bringing back memories, stirring feelings. She was grieving. And crying.

When he'd seen the moisture brighten her eyes, he'd wanted to pull her into his arms, hug her and reassure her that everything would be okay. That Hattie had moved on to a better place, that they would find the locket, that Sebastian would wind up behind bars as he so well deserved.

He kept his hands glued to the steering

wheel, his foot firmly on the gas. While he was still her comforter, he'd taken on a new role last night. One he didn't intend to let her forget as easily as she wanted to. He'd become her lover, and now he wanted her to admit that she was *in* love with him.

For whatever reason, she refused to see the truth. She feared it.

Because she's got a husband, buddy.

True, but she didn't love Sebastian. He'd seen it in her eyes—the pain and fear and regret whenever she spoke of him. No, she didn't love Sebastian.

But did she love him?

He wouldn't have thought so, but he'd seen the way she'd looked at him when he was wounded. She'd been more than concerned, she just didn't want to admit it because of circumstance, and fear.

Regardless, Dylan wanted to share the future with Julie and Thomas. He wanted to be more than her friend.

The ruts in the dirt road jerked him back to reality and the rickety cabin barely visible just beyond the trees.

"There it is." She leaned forward in her seat

and stared over the dash. "It looks the same. For the most part."

He noticed the large spray of wilting flowers standing out front.

In Memory of Hattie.

"There are her potted plants." She indicated the row of pots lining the porch as she climbed out and leaned into the back seat of the car to retrieve Thomas. Each bowl sprouted a different flower, the colors ranging from pink to orange, red to yellow. "She loved flowers," she said as she cradled her son. "And Jake." Her gaze shifted to the pig lazing on the porch steps. "She loved him more than any creature on this earth. Just so long as he stayed out of her onion patch."

The dusty pink animal wore a collar from which a small leather square hung suspended with his name printed on it.

"Nadine?" Her gaze shifted to the old black woman, her hair snow-white and her face creased with wrinkles, who sat in the rocker. Wood creaked and groaned as Nadine pushed with her feet and the chair moved. She'd been Hattie's nearest neighbor, her arch enemy at times and her best friend at others. They'd grown up together on the bayou, and Julie knew Nadine nearly as well as she knew Hattie.

"She's gone," the woman said before pushing up from the rocker and pulling Julie into her arms for a hug.

"I know," Julie murmured against the woman's shoulder. "I'm so sorry."

"I don't know what I'm gonna do without her. Why, she could play Bingo better than anybody over at the church. One time I saw her handle twenty cards during one game." She wiped at her tears with a wadded-up handkerchief. "They messed up her place." Nadine motioned to the broken chair that sat on the far edge of the porch, along with a box of trash. "I cleaned the place up as best I could, but they done went and broke a mess of stuff. Damn kids."

"Kids?"

"Sheriff says the damage was more than likely caused by the kids that pirogue down the bayou and smoke dope in the swamp. Says they needed money for drugs and decided to ransack Hattie's place. She got caught in the cross fire."

"Do they have any suspects?"

"You know Sheriff Benoit. If he does, he ain't sayin'. And if he doesn't, he ain't admit-tin' as much. That man never thinks he's wrong.'' Nadine leaned down to pet Jake. ''Thank God this little fella kept his nose out of it. He was hidin' under the house when I got here. Hattie would never be able to leave this world in peace if something had happened to Jake.'' She wiped at more of her tears. ''I'm so glad you're here, child. She sure did take a hankerin' to you and your boy.'' She smiled tearfully at Thomas, who gurgled a greeting. ''My, but he's getting as round and fat as Jake, here.''

At her words, Julie smiled, and the sight sent a warmth surging through Dylan. ''Finally. He's feeling a lot better.''

''I heard he got pneumonia.''

Julie nodded. ''He was pretty sick for a while. But he's a healthy, happy baby now.''

''And what about you?'' Nadine studied her a long moment before a knowing smile curled her lips. ''You're doing better, too.'' She winked. ''I see you finally took Hattie's advice and found yourself a handsome beau.''

''This is Dylan. He's a good friend of mine.''

Dylan had heard the words time and time again in the past, and they'd always bothered him. No more. Now they simply fueled his determination to prove her wrong.

He would. When all was said and done and Sebastian was a bad memory, he would prove Julie Cooper wrong once and for all, and then he would marry her and never let her go.

Just a friend.

Maybe she was right. And maybe not. It was a chance Dylan was willing to take.

He glanced around him at the trees crowding the clearing, their trunks layered with lichens, their limbs covered with trailing fingers of Spanish moss.

Despite the temperature, a tremor traveled over his skin as he noted the isolated location. He could see why Julie had thought Hattie's a great place to hide. Now, however, with Sebastian hot on their trail, his only thought was that she could scream her head off and nobody would hear her but the alligators.

He slid his arm around her shoulder. "We need to hurry."

"Funeral's not until this afternoon," Nadine said. "No need to run off. We could visit till then."

"I didn't come for the funeral." Julie swallowed. "I wish I could stay. I would stay, but

I can't. Hattie was holding something for me, Nadine. Something really important. Did she mention it to you?''

''She's got that photo of you and Thomas hanging in her kitchen. But that's the only thing I know of.''

''No, it wasn't the photo. It was a piece of jewelry. I need to find it.''

The old woman nodded before settling back in the rocking chair once again and putting the piece of grass back between her teeth. ''Look away, child. If it's that important to you, Hattie would want you to find it.''

''Thanks, ma'am.'' Dylan steered Julie through the doorway and inside the small cabin.

''This is it,'' she said, her gaze sweeping the room.

Dylan followed suit. The cabin was sparsely furnished. There was a wrought-iron double bed, a rickety table with four straw-backed chairs and a faded lime-green sofa. The furniture had obviously been broken and the sofa slashed, but Nadine had worked hard at patching it back together. Off to the side sat a black iron cookstove, a small sink with a rust stain around the drain and a row of shelves lined with teacups.

Julie went straight for the cups and fingered the collection. "She loved these, too. She collected them. I remember when one girl who came to Hattie for help—Denise, I think her name was—couldn't pay. Hattie said never mind. Just bring her a teacup when she could. That's what she asked all of us." Julie touched a rose patterned cup with a scarred gold rim. "I brought her this. I picked it up at a resale shop in town after Hattie planted rosebushes in the back. She had a thing for yellow roses, and when I saw this, I knew she would like it."

Julie trailed her finger on the edge of the saucer and remembered Hattie's smile, her soft gaze, her strong hands, her stubborn resolve. She remembered everything that had made the old midwife such a wonderful and unique woman, and she wished yet again that she could turn back the clock and do something to save her dear friend.

"I'm so sorry," she breathed. Tears burned the backs of her eyes and she blinked frantically.

"It's pretty." Dylan's voice soothed the anguish that tore at her heart. His hand closed over her shoulder and he squeezed, drawing her back to reality and comforting her at the same time. For a split second, she wanted to turn into his warmth, feel his arms tighten around her and simply cry.

For Hattie, because her life had been cut far too short. For Thomas, because he'd been robbed of a normal childhood. For Dylan, because he'd been sucked into something far too dangerous for his own good. For herself, because she'd caused so much pain for so many people. It was her fault Hattie had died. Her fault Thomas was on the run. Her fault Dylan had nearly gotten killed.

Because she'd misjudged Sebastian in the first place.

You started it and you can stop it.

The voice whispered through her head and filled her with a sense of courage. She fought back her fear and dread and guilt and stiffened. "We need to look in each one of these cups. She might have put it in one of them."

They searched through all of the cups that hadn't been broken in the struggle, and after that, they looked in various jars and tin cans containing everything from flour to tobacco, until they'd searched every nook and cranny where Hattie might have hidden the locket. Even the trunk beneath the floor held nothing but old photographs and a wad of money, which Julie handed to Nadine. "For Hattie's girls," she told the old woman.

Hattie's girls were a group of women who'd "graduated" from Hattie's place. They'd come to her pregnant, down and out, and the old woman had helped them. They'd stayed around after the births of their babies. They'd moved into town and stayed close by to be near the woman who'd given them hope when they'd had nothing else. They traveled around to nearby churches and schools, counseling teens and doing their best to keep other young girls from following in their footsteps.

Two hours later, Julie had exhausted every possible hiding place. She sank down on the edge of the bed next to Jake, who sprawled on a patchwork quilt, and pulled Thomas into her arms. The baby smiled up at her, completely oblivious to her frustration. As if all were right with the world and their future didn't hinge on one tiny piece of jewelry.

What if it didn't?

She ignored the doubt. The locket meant something to Sebastian. Something important enough to warrant murder. Something important enough to keep her looking even when she'd run out of places.

Dylan hadn't been having much luck, either. He'd dug in each and every flowerpot on the front porch and poked around the backyard, looking under Hattie's wheelbarrow, in her chicken coop. At the moment, Julie could see him digging through Hattie's garden on the long shot that the old woman had hidden it among her patch of Vidalia onions.

"Where is it?" Julie asked Jake as she stroked his head with her free hand and patted Thomas with her other. "You know, don't you, Jake? You saw her hide it, didn't you?"

Great. Now she was talking to a pig. Talk about desperate.

She fingered Jake's collar and traced the small leather square. It wasn't merely a name badge as she'd first thought, but a pouch with a small flap that hung from the collar. Red embroidery spelled out his name.

"It has to be here," she said as she mindlessly traced the edge of the pouch. "But where? Hattie wouldn't have put it just anywhere. It would be someplace safe. Someplace special."

Or with *someone* special, she decided as she noted the lump in Jake's pouch.

Of course. Hattie had loved Jake. He was always with her, always close. *Special.*

Excitement rushed through her as she opened the pouch. Sliding two fingers in, she pulled out the contents, a smile spreading across her face as the locket came into full view.

The metal was warm against her palm and she sent up a silent prayer to Hattie for being so clever. No wonder Sebastian's men hadn't been able to find the locket. Who would have thought to look on a pig?

Relief washed through her, along with a rush of excitement. She jumped to her feet.

"Dylan!" she cried as she rushed out onto the porch with Thomas on one hip and the locket clasped in her free hand. *"Dylan!"* She waved toward the garden.

A few seconds later, a head popped up, followed by the rest of his body. He smiled at her, but then the expression faded as his gaze flicked to a point just beyond her left shoulder.

She couldn't help herself, she smiled, feeling for the first time, deep in her heart, that maybe things would turn out all right. "It's here," she said, hoping to stir his excitement. "I found it!"

"Nice going." She heard Sebastian's words a heartbeat before she felt the cold press of metal at her throat.

CHAPTER TEN

SEBASTIAN'S HAND closed around Julie's arm and he yanked her back toward him. The knife pressed deeper into her throat and fear lurched through her. Thomas stirred in her arms at the sudden movement and she held her baby closer.

Fear filled her, yet at the same time, she felt a fierce sense of protectiveness. Her mothering instinct kept her heart calm when it otherwise would have raced ninety to nothing with panic. She had to be smart enough to keep her son out of harm's way.

To keep him out of Sebastian's way.

"Well, well, you found it."

"I don't know what you're talking about."

"Come, now, Julie. You just ran out here yelling about finding the locket and now you're trying to tell me you didn't?"

"I was yelling, but not about any locket. I found something of Hattie's. An old picture."

"That's what you have in your hand?"

Her fingers tightened around the locket. "I don't have anything in my hand."

"Sure you do." He pressed the knife deeper. "Don't you?"

She wanted to throw the locket at him and beg him to let her go free, but he wouldn't. He would never let her go. Now, without the locket, Julie had nothing to bargain with.

"I see you brought our friend into this," Sebastian said as he motioned toward Dylan, who stepped up onto the porch.

"She didn't drag me into anything. I came willingly. We're friends."

"You always did have a thing for her."

"The three of us were friends. What happened, Sebastian?"

At Dylan's calm voice, Julie nearly screamed until she realized what he was doing. With each question he took a small step forward, closing the distance inch by inch.

"Nothing happened. I'm making a living, end of story."

"You've got enough money to last the average person a few lifetimes."

"I'm not the average person, and it's not just about money. It's about really *living*. About having all the advantages and using them to get what I want." He smiled. "Nobody does it better than me, you know. I win because I know how to play the game, to turn every disadvantage into an advantage. To do any and everything to ensure that I win."

"You won't win this time," Julie told him.

"Spoken like someone who's never played the game. Listen, sweetheart, I *will* win," he said, pressing the knife against her throat and making her swallow. The blade cut into her and she felt a drop of blood slide down her neck. "Because I hold all the cards, or I soon will. Now hand over the locket."

"You heard the lady. She doesn't have it."

"Stop right there," he said to Dylan, who'd been about to take another step forward. "I mean it." He held Julie tighter, the blade pushing so hard she dared not swallow for fear that the cold metal would slice into her jugular. "You're lying," he murmured into Julie's ears. "You've gotten really good at that this past year, honey."

She drew in a slow, steady breath. As she relaxed, Sebastian's hold seemed to ease enough for her to speak. "I had to," she croaked.

"I had quite a time finding you at first. You covered your tracks, hid your identity."

"But you still found me."

"I took a guess and tracked down Hattie. I sent three of my friends to pay her a visit. You had a little run-in with one of them yesterday."

The man who'd knifed Dylan in the parking lot.

"He didn't handle that job quite so successfully," Sebastian observed dryly.

Julie hugged Thomas even closer. Grief welled inside her, fueling her courage and her anger. "You killed Hattie."

"I already said I didn't. My men did. Not intentionally, mind you. They just got a little carried away. Once the old woman was gone, I figured it was time to track down my loving wife."

"I'm not your wife," Julie protested. "And you're not my husband. You haven't been for a long, long time."

"That hurts me, Julie. And here I was worried sick about you when you left."

"Worried that I would tell the police about you and your dealings with J. B. Crowe."

He laughed. "That was the last thing I worried about. It would have been your word against mine without proof.''

''But I have proof.'' Her fingers tightened around the locket.

He laughed. ''You're catching on. Why else would I follow you out to this godforsaken place?''

''What's the proof, Sebastian? Did you put something in my locket?''

Sebastian was silent.

''I'm right, then. So what is it?''

''Wouldn't you like me to tell you.''

''Why not?'' Julie was stalling for time, desperately searching for some way to escape. ''I'm not getting out of here alive, am I, so what difference does it make?''

He seemed to weigh her words. ''True.''

''Then tell me. I'm anxious to see exactly how clever you are.'' Though her question wouldn't have been enough to make him reveal the truth, her flattery stroked his ego.

''Forget clever, honey. It's ingenious. No one would suspect that an old piece of jewelry like that would contain a microchip.''

''A microchip?''

''Implanted in the back. But it doesn't tie me

to anything. It implicates someone much more dangerous.''

"That someone being Luke Silva," Dylan said, inching forward. "Isn't that right?

"You always were pretty sharp, Garrett. It's a shame you didn't put that head of yours to good use instead of letting it all go to waste chasing bad guys."

"I wouldn't say that's a waste. It's not the most high-paying job, but it's a rush to lock up scumbags like you."

"A scumbag? Is that any way to talk to your best friend?''

"We're not friends."

Sebastian's gaze narrowed. "No, I guess we're not, considering you're sleeping with my wife."

"She's hardly your wife any longer, and you're not her husband. You don't know how to be a husband."

"And I suppose you do?" He smirked. "I never figured you one to settle for sloppy seconds, but then again, she is rather pretty. Still a looker like back in our college days, eh, Dylan?''

"Let her go."

"No problem." The knife sliced deeper and

fire shot through Julie. The pain blindsided her and her hold on Thomas loosened. Before she knew what was happening, she found the baby yanked from her arms.

"Thomas—no!" Julie reached for Thomas and the locket fell from her grasp.

Sebastian's free hand landed upside her head and she reeled to the side as he snatched up the locket.

"Game's over," Sebastian said, the locket and child in hand.

"No!" Julie cried as she grabbed for Thomas, but Sebastian stepped back, pointing a gun in her direction.

"Come any closer and you put your baby at risk."

Julie froze, stunned as much by the cold fury in Sebastian's eyes as the gun in his hand.

"Maybe it's time little Thomas and I have a chance to get to know each other," Sebastian said, holding the baby in front of him.

Julie felt Dylan tense beside her but she willed him not to move, not to jeopardize her baby's life. Standing helplessly, she watched silently as Sebastian disappeared behind the cabin. Seconds later, the sound of a car engine broke the stillness.

"Dear God," Julie breathed, watching Sebastian's car flash through the veils of Spanish moss, headed for the dirt road. The roar of another engine sounded nearby.

"Get in." Dylan pulled up beside her in his car and hauled her inside. A few seconds later, they sped down the road after Sebastian and Thomas.

"Hold on," he said as he took a winding turn and the car tilted onto two wheels.

"Hurry. I can't see him. I can't see the car. I can't see my baby!"

This couldn't be happening. The thought flashed through her mind as panic beat at her senses. Sebastian had Thomas. He had her baby!

For the next few heart-pounding moments as the car careered down the old dirt road, Julie held on for dear life. Her own and her child's. "Please. We have to catch him," she cried. "We have to."

"We will," Dylan vowed, but just then a deep rut sent the car swerving toward the right. A tree rushed at them and slammed into the front grille. Julie was aware of two things happening at once—the air bag exploded and her head slammed against the side window.

"Don't hurt my baby." The desperate prayer was Julie's last conscious thought before her vision faded and everything went black.

"I FOUND HIM."

"Excellent."

"Not so excellent. I found him, but then lost him."

Silence settled as Mikey waited for a response. When he didn't get one, he rushed on, his voice nervous, fearful.

Rightly so. Luke was angry.

"Cooper was furious that Pendleton let Garrett and his wife go," Mikey blurted. "I—I think Cooper wanted Pendleton to conduct a little interrogation before Garrett and the woman reached that old midwife's cabin. It didn't work. The woman practically ran him over. Anyhow, I followed Pendleton to Cooper. The man was not happy. He headed out to Devereaux's cabin himself and intercepted the two of them."

"And?"

"All hell broke loose. Cooper ended up running away with the kid. I guess he figured his wife would keep quiet to protect her son. She and Garrett went after him, but they had an accident.''

''What happened?''

''I didn't hang around to see. I tailed Cooper as far as I could, but he was going too fast and the road was too rough. I couldn't keep up and so I lost him.''

''Find him,'' Luke said after a long silent moment. ''Understand?''

''Yes, sir,'' came Mikey's frightened voice.

Fear was good. Fear got results. Luke thrived on instilling the emotion in his subordinates. It was the only way to command their respect, as well as their loyalty.

''Find him,'' he repeated. *''Now.''*

A DRUM BEAT at Julie's temple, so loud and deafening she winced with each strike. She wanted to open her eyes. She needed to, but it hurt. She let the darkness pull her back into painless oblivion.

''Julie.''

The sound of her name drew her forward, back toward the pounding and the pain and the man who waited at her bedside.

She forced her eyes open, wincing at the overhead light that threatened to blind her. All her effort concentrated on breathing. Each ragged breath echoed in her head and made her temples hurt.

"Can you hear me, Julie? Come on, baby. Talk to me."

Through the black fog suspended above her, she saw him. Dylan. He leaned over her, concern bright in his blue eyes. She wanted to keep her eyes open, to talk to him.

She couldn't.

He turned away and she heard another voice.

"It's just a minor concussion. She'll be okay, but she'll have one hell of a headache. She's lucky the airbag released. At the speed you were going, the injuries sustained would have been much more severe. Yours, too. Speaking of which, I'd really like to get an X ray of your ribs. Just in case."

"I'm fine," Dylan said.

The sound of his voice compelled her to open her eyes once again. This time, she concentrated, forcing her lids up.

Blinking at the fluorescent lights, she tried to hold back the tears that instantly welled up. The lights brightened then dimmed, brightened then dimmed, matching the frenzied tempo of the drumming in her head.

Concussion? Impact? Injuries?

The questions raced through her mind a frenzied moment before reality hit and she remembered the car chase. The crash.

"Thomas." Julie raised herself up a fraction. She had to find her baby. To help him.

She teetered to the side as white splotches danced in front of her. Slumping back to the pillow, she squeezed her eyes shut for one brief, calming moment, praying for strength. She had to get her composure and pull herself together. She had to go after her baby.

"When will she wake up?" Dylan asked.

She opened her eyes again focusing on the narrow hospital bed. There he stood, his face grave, his eyes guarded—completely in control as usual. She wondered if she had imagined the distraught look on his face, the anxiety in his voice when he'd pleaded with her in the car. Maybe she'd had a delusion—a crazy, pain-filled delusion.

"Dylan," she murmured. He turned toward her. The moment her gaze locked with his, there was no mistaking the worry and anguish, and something else—a spark that warmed her and chased the shivering chills away for a brief moment before Julie remembered that she didn't believe in sparks.

She'd stopped believing a long time ago when her love for Sebastian had turned out to be her worst nightmare. She'd been so wrong then.

But no more. She was older and wiser and she wasn't going that route again. She wouldn't risk the special friendship she had with Dylan Garrett.

Too late, a voice whispered as a vision of their night together pushed to the forefront of her mind.

"It looks like she's awake," said the man standing next to Dylan. Dressed in a white coat with a stethoscope draped about his neck, he gripped a clipboard in one hand while the other rested in his pocket. "I'll just leave you two," he said.

"So you finally decided to open your eyes?" Dylan asked once the doctor had left.

"Yes…" she murmured. "How long have I been out?"

"A few hours. You were knocked unconscious in the crash. I carried you to the main road." At his words, she noted the sling hanging around his neck, cradling one of his arms.

"It's not broken," he said, as if reading her thoughts. "I pulled the ligaments in my shoulder and the sling is to help keep everything stable. A trucker passed us on the road and called an ambulance. You were out the entire time."

"My head hurts," she said, closing her eyes.

"But you're okay," he reminded her. "Luckily, the wound to your neck was superficial." A nerve-wrenching silence ensued as he studied her.

"What about my baby?"

"Thomas will be all right. Sebastian's dangerous, but I can't believe he would go as far as to..." He shifted and glanced away.

"Go on and say it." Her gaze locked with his. "Say what you're thinking."

"Okay." He held her stare. "I don't think he'll kill him."

"How could you doubt it after what he did today? After what he had his men do to Hattie?"

Another thought struck her. "Oh my God, what about Nadine and the other girls who were back at Hattie's? Did Sebastian...?"

Dylan rested a hand on hers to calm her. "It's okay. When Nadine saw Sebastian sneak up on you with a knife, she jumped in the pi-

rogue and went downriver to notify the sheriff.''

Julie shook her head, still not quite able to
believe what had happened. "I never would
have thought... I mean, I knew Sebastian was
dangerous, but to use his own baby..."

"Thomas is the ticket to your cooperation,"
Dylan reminded her. "Sebastian wants your silence, he knows you'll do whatever he says as
long as he has Thomas."

"Which isn't going to be for long. We're going after him."

"No, we're not. I am."

"If you think I'm staying here while you run
after him, you've got another think coming."

"Why do you have to be so damned difficult?"

"Because," she snapped, then her anger
faded into guilt and heartache and her voice
softened. "Because it's my fault. I risked
Thomas's life. If anything happens..."

"Nothing's going to happen. I swear, Julie.
I won't let anything happen. Not to you. Not to
Thomas."

For the first time since she'd opened her
eyes, she noticed his damp shirt and wet hair.

His face looked haggard. Fine lines etched the corners of his eyes.

She reached out and touched his face. His skin was warm and stubbly beneath her fingertips. "I don't know what I would do without you, Dylan." She traced his bottom lip with her fingertip and let herself imagine what forever would be like with such a man—*this* man—if only circumstances had been different. If she'd lived her life differently and made other choices.

But she hadn't, and so she let her hand fall away, refusing to think about what might have been. "You're a good friend, Dylan."

"No, I'm not." He turned away from her, leaving her to wonder what he meant.

"So, what do we do?" She emphasized the *we,* determined to let him know that she wasn't going to stay behind.

She couldn't. Not with her child's life hanging in the balance.

She expected an argument, but he said nothing. He simply turned and eyed her for a long moment before he shrugged. "We get smart, that's what we do. We're not going to find ourselves in the very same situation again, with just Thomas and the two of us." He ran his good hand through his hair. "We need help, Julie."

"The police?"

"Not just any police. Zach Logan."

CHAPTER ELEVEN

EARLY THE NEXT MORNING Dylan walked into the office of the chief of detectives at the Dallas Police Department. A distinguished-looking man with dark hair and a mustache sat behind a large desk overflowing with paperwork and stained coffee cups.

Zach Logan had been Dylan's boss when he'd worked for the department. Zach was still involved in an undercover operation to bring down the local mob, and only a few months ago Dylan had helped his former boss identify Sebastian, who'd been spotted by Zach's men on J. B. Crowe's estate.

Now it was Dylan's turn to ask for help.

"This meeting is about more than catching up on old times, isn't it?" Zach asked, getting up to shake Dylan's hand.

Dylan nodded. "I need your help, buddy." That's why he'd hightailed it to Dallas when the doctor had discharged Julie from the hospital late last night. She'd wanted to go back to San Antonio, but he'd convinced her that they needed help. Sebastian could flee the country if he wanted to and they would never know. They needed resources to make sure he didn't leave. Otherwise, they would never find Thomas.

Fear rippled through him, but he pushed it aside. They *would* find Thomas. He'd found each and every person he'd ever set out to look for, and he didn't intend to break his record now. Not when Thomas meant more to him than anyone he'd yet to search for.

Except Julie, that is.

His ex-boss had been his best bet. After thirty years in law enforcement, Zach Logan had connections, especially when it came to the mob. Dylan had called and set up a meeting with the detective the second he'd rolled into town.

"What's up?" Zach asked as he settled back in his chair.

"It's Cooper," Dylan stated.

Zach eyed him closely. "We've been trying to get something on him for months."

Dylan's voice was hard. "I think I can help you there—how about a couple of charges— murder and kidnapping?"

Zach straightened in his chair. "Okay, buddy, you've got my full attention."

Dylan quickly filled Zach in on Julie's situation, starting with the day she heard Sebastian talking with Luke Silva and went into hiding, afraid for her life and that of her baby. He told Zach of Hattie's murder and Sebastian's attempt to harm Julie for the locket.

"Once he had the locket, he basically kidnapped their eight-month-old son to ensure Julie's silence," Dylan finished.

"She file any charges?"

"She filed a missing persons report, but technically she can't finger him for kidnapping because he's the kid's father."

"No court orders granting her custody?"

Dylan shook his head. "She couldn't file for divorce or custody. She was living on the run. Hiding. Any legal proceedings would have led him right to her."

"The hiding's obviously over," Zach said after hearing Dylan out. "She should file for temporary custody right now. I can talk to Judge Mayfield over in family court. She'll hear it right away, considering the circumstances. At least that will give Julie legal grounds to press kidnapping charges and get the police involved in the abduction.''

''Thanks.'' Dylan ran a hand through his hair. ''Then what?''

''We find him,'' Zach said as he reached for the phone. ''You think he's in San Antonio?''

''Maybe. He's got resources. He could skip the country. But that would defeat the purpose. He's got the info he needs in the locket, and if he's using the kid as bait, he'll want to be accessible so that Julie will come to him. He's got to be hoping she won't go to the cops and risk Thomas's life.''

Zach nodded. ''Makes sense. I've got some friends on the San Antonio force. I'll call and fill them in.''

''I'm going there first thing tomorrow and start looking myself.''

''That's a good idea. Make Julie's presence known. Maybe you'll get lucky and Cooper will come after her again and expose himself.''

''I'm not endangering her safety. I'll find him myself.''

''And what are you going to do?''

''What are you driving at?''

''You're not on the force anymore, Dylan. You can't arrest him. You need the authorities for that. And you need someone even bigger to make it stick. Cooper has major connections. The local authorities aren't going to be enough to press a case against him. You need the big boys for that."

"The FBI?"

Zach reached for the phone. "The one and only."

"YOU CALLED the FBI?" Julie held the receiver and listened to Dylan's voice float over the line.

"I didn't, darlin'. That was Zach's decision. Sebastian's a powerful man. If we want him to pay for what he's done, what he's doing right now, we need to go all the way to the top. The Feds jumped right on this. They've been after Crowe's entire organization. J.B.'s still running the show from prison. They've nabbed a few of the players, but they're missing some key people like Sebastian and Luke Silva. This will give them the chance to bring Sebastian in and, if they can find the locket, the proof they need to put Crowe, Silva and him away for a long, long time."

"What about Thomas?" Her fingers tightened around the receiver as memories flashed in her mind. Sebastian holding Thomas. Sebastian holding the knife. "He can't get away with this."

"He won't, which is why I'm calling. At this point, it's not kidnapping. Not until we see a lawyer and you file for custody. Now." He gave her the address for the courthouse and told her who to see. "Zach's already called the judge and she'll hear the plea right away. All you have to do is show up and tell your story."

"What about you?" She hated to sound so needy, but the past few hours spent pacing the hotel room had taken its toll. Her nerves were frazzled, her emotions raging like a Gulf hurricane. "Are you going to meet me there?"

"I can't. The Feds need written details on everything that's happened since you went on the run. I have to fill them in. I'll call you if they need to talk with you. Otherwise I'll meet you back at the hotel later." There were no words of comfort. Dylan seemed distant, as if he were trying to hold back.

As if he regretted their night together and wished he could turn back the clock.

"Thanks for everything you're doing."

"Don't mention it." The dial tone floated over the line before Julie could respond and tell him half the things racing through her mind.

How sorry she felt. How appreciative she was. How much in love—

She forced aside the last thought. It was too late to start believing now. She wasn't going to let emotion rule her decisions ever again. If she'd been logical where Sebastian had been concerned, she would have seen him for the man he was—competitive, heartless. A fake.

Never again. She and Dylan were friends. Nothing more.

The trouble was, she feared they weren't even that after what had happened. And judging by his aloofness, she was right.

One of her worst fears had been realized. Julie had lost her best friend.

The truth haunted her for the next few hours as she went to the courthouse and filed for temporary custody. When she returned to the empty hotel room and crawled into the shower, she let the tears come.

They blurred her vision as she stood beneath the scalding spray and prayed for everything to be all right. If only she could erase the past forty-eight hours. She should have listened to Dylan and gone into hiding. Thomas would be with her and the night with Dylan would never have happened.

She would have her best friend back.

She needed her friend back.

Julie slumped against the tiled wall of the shower. Hot water sluiced over her shoulders, streamed down her back and buttocks to race in swirling rivulets across the white marble basin and disappear down the drain.

If only she could disappear as easily, she thought. But she couldn't, nor could she erase her one night with Dylan. Even now, with the water prickling her sensitive skin, she could still feel his hands, his mouth...

God, what had she done?

She'd ruined everything, and all for a night of pleasure.

But it had been more. Dylan made her feel whole, complete. He eased her troubled soul and gave her a sort of peace she'd been searching for, yet unable to find. Dylan didn't just rouse her hormones. He stirred something much deeper...something much more threatening to her sanity.

Crazy. She was imagining things to soothe her conscience. To excuse her actions. She'd messed up, plain and simple.

All the way around.

Her thoughts went to Thomas and her tears

spilled over again. With a trembling hand, she turned the chrome shower knob. The water slowed to a dribble, then stopped.

Minutes later, Julie wrapped herself in a white terry-cloth bathrobe and walked into the bedroom. It was late afternoon and the sun was setting. She headed over to the sliding doors, pushed one panel of glass aside and stepped out onto the balcony. Orange edged the Dallas skyline.

It was a beautiful sight. One she would have appreciated if her thoughts hadn't been in such chaos. Despite the warm temperature, a chill worked its way through her and she wrapped her arms around her chest.

A drop of water slid down her cheek from her wet hair, which hung in dripping tendrils around her face. Staring at the street below, she watched the cars race back and forth. The world moved on as if nothing had happened.

As if all was calm and Julie's heart wasn't breaking.

Thomas. She thought of him, his smiling face and his chubby arms and legs. She ached to feel his warmth and smell his baby scent.

She'd never been a baby person. Never oohed and ahhed over other people's children.

She liked kids, but they were a bit of an unknown entity. After all, she'd been an only child with no younger siblings. She'd never been around babies. While the news of her impending pregnancy had been wonderful, she'd been frightened as well as overjoyed.

Would she be a good mother?

Her fears had been fed by the fact that she didn't have a normal pregnancy. There'd been no trips to the ice-cream shop to indulge special cravings. No shopping sprees at the local mall. Her life had centered solely around survival.

The pregnancy had been stressful and the actual birth even more so. But the moment she'd stared down at her child, all her fears had faded away. She'd felt such pure happiness, unlike anything she'd ever experienced before. And peace. Despite the uncertainty of her existence, she'd been calm. She'd known just how to touch him, to hold him, to kiss him.

She'd been a mother, with all its worries and responsibilities, and all its joys.

Joy. That's what Thomas gave her. What she wanted to give back to him.

Instead, she'd shown him nothing but danger and peril. And now Sebastian had him.

Julie was so lost in her worries that she didn't

hear the footsteps behind her. She heard only his voice, low and husky and so very disconcerting, and a ripple of awareness wafted through her.

"Are you all right?"

She closed her eyes. *Yes!* her mind screamed. *Now that you're here.* But she could only nod her head. She would make it. She had to make it.

She hugged her arms tighter to dispel the chills. If only they would go away and she could pull herself together.

Dylan came up behind her, as if her thoughts had lured him closer, but he didn't touch her.

He wouldn't touch her.

Not ever, ever again.

"I have temporary custody," she told him.

"Good. Everything's set up with the Feds. They're already watching Sebastian's place in San Antonio. If he goes home, we'll know, and if he tries to leave the country, we'll know."

"So what do we do now?"

"We go back to San Antonio and we wait."

She shook her head and shivered. It was cold. Too cold. "I don't think I can. I have to do something. I have to find him."

"And do what? You don't know where he's

at, and even if you manage to find him on your own, you'll only put Thomas's life in greater danger. If you show up gunning for Sebastian without any backup, chances are he'll kill you. And then he'll have no use for Thomas.''

"Thomas is his son."

"Yes, and that might make a difference."

She remembered the coldness in Sebastian's eyes, the way he'd held the knife at her throat. "It won't make any difference." She drew in a deep breath and walked to the window. "God, I hate this. I hate him."

"You don't hate anybody, Julie. You can't. It'll eat you up inside." He moved beside her, as if oblivious to the tremors that racked her body. "All we can do is wait and let the Feds do their job."

"I know." She touched his hand, but he pulled away and her shivers grew worse. "I'm sorry."

"Would you stop saying that? I don't want your apologies." His voice grew gruff, his eyes dark and stormy. "I want you."

She shook her head. "I don't want you to want me."

"Then what do you want?"

"I want my friend back."

"That's not possible. I know you want me, Julie." His voice was so calm, so sure, chipping at the barrier she tried desperately to erect between them. "I can see it every time I look at you. If you can tell me it's not true and mean it, I'll never bring the subject up again. You can forget that night."

"But you won't."

"I can't. I don't want to. And I don't think you want to, either." His lips were so close to her ear now, too close for comfort.

And comfort was all that she wanted from him.

"That night shouldn't have happened. There's too much in my past for this to work. And the future... It's all too crazy."

"You're thinking too much. Sometimes you have to trust your instincts."

"Me? Are you kidding? I failed Instinct 101, remember? I thought I married a man who loved me, when in reality he only loved himself."

"You were barely eighteen when you met him. You didn't know what love was."

"And now I do?"

"I think you do." Their gazes locked and she knew what he was talking about. As much as it thrilled her, it also filled her with a sense of panic and fear.

"Can't you just hold me?" She shook her head as the tears spilled over. "Can't you just hold me and tell me everything will be okay? Can't you just be my friend? That's what I need right now." She put her back to him and gave in to the tears burning in her eyes. "If you could just be my friend."

A few seconds later, she felt his chest, strong and warm, at her back. "Is that what you want? What you *really* want?"

She nodded.

"Okay," he replied, his voice gruff, tinged with a thread of sadness that niggled at something deep inside her. He tilted her chin to capture her gaze with his own, his eyes flashing blue fire in the waning sunlight. "I'm your friend."

"Thank you," she said as she slid her arms around him. He pulled her close and Julie relished the feeling.

Dylan's warmth chased away the chills and filled her with a sense of comfort unlike anything she'd ever felt before.

She wasn't sure when her feelings changed. She only knew that the warmth quickly turned to something more as he stroked his hand up and down her back. It was meant to be soothing, but her heart hammered and her nerves buzzed and need flowered deep in her belly.

She realized then that Dylan could never go back to being just a friend.

She wouldn't settle for it because she wanted more.

She wanted everything where this man was concerned.

"I'm so sorry," she murmured, the enormity of her feelings overwhelming her in that instant.

"I'm tired of hearing that. You're not putting my life in danger. I'm here willingly. I—"

"That's not what I mean." She pulled away and stared up into his eyes. "I'm sorry for everything. All along, it was you and I didn't see it."

"What do you mean?"

"You were the one, Dylan. Not Sebastian. Never Sebastian. I just didn't see it. I was so stupid, I didn't see the truth. Deep down, I felt it though, but I didn't trust my feelings. Not then and not now."

"Forget the past. It's over and done with. There's just now. Today."

"Tonight," she corrected as she loosened her belt and let the robe fall open.

When his fingers found her taut nipples, she relaxed against him, forgetting everything except his feverish touch.

"The past is past," he repeated again, making everything seem so simple.

It wasn't. Nothing about her life was simple anymore, and Dylan made things all the more complicated. But his presence was so overwhelming, the attraction between them so magnetic, she knew she could forget, at least for the moment.

"The past is past," she echoed, taking a deep breath.

Dylan's attention focused on the rise and fall of her chest. "Are you okay?" he asked, the question lighting his eyes. "You look flushed. Are you hot?"

She'd been cold before, but now she felt as if she were burning. She could only nod, and her breath caught when he reached out to trail his finger up her bare thigh to the hemline bunched near her hips.

Dylan's gaze held hers as he slipped the robe off her shoulders, trailed his hands down her arms to her waist. She felt herself throb when he brushed the thin material of her panties.

"Yes, it definitely is hot out here," he murmured.

With his fingers he tugged her lace panties down. They slid over her legs, past her ankles, then he tossed them on the floor beside her.

"A little cooler?" he asked, heat spiraling from the deep blue depths of his eyes, making her burn hotter.

She shook her head.

He lifted her into his arms and walked back into the hotel room. Easing her down onto the bed, he knelt in front of her parted legs. Bending her knees, he spread his hands on the insides of her thighs and urged them open to his smoldering gaze. His hands slid higher....

When he touched her moist heat, parted the sensitive flesh and slipped a finger inside, she felt the air rush from her lungs. Her limbs turned to liquid. She tilted her head back, a low moan escaping her lips.

"It's hot in here, too," he said, pushing deeper, caressing, stoking the fire that burned inside her. When he leaned down and touched his lips to the inside of one knee, letting his tongue follow the same path as his hand, higher, higher, she wound her fingers in his hair.

"Please," she cried, needing to feel the heat of his mouth.

"I thought you just wanted me to hold you," he reminded her, his lips a steady vibration on her smooth flesh. The sensation sent white-hot flames shooting through her veins.

"I do." Her gaze locked with his for a long moment and she knew he needed to hear the words again. The truth she'd been denying for so long. "I want that and more."

He grinned before dipping his head again. His mouth found her and she cried out, holding him to her as he flicked his tongue over the swollen flesh. Julie tossed her head from side to side, eager for the rapture only he could give her. She bucked against him, racing toward the blinding light. Then suddenly, without warning, her flight halted.

Dylan pulled away.

After several moments, she opened her eyes to find him poised above her, intense, watchful.

"Almost?" he asked, trailing one finger over her bottom lip. She tasted herself on him and felt the heat inside her flame hotter.

"Yes..." she breathed.

He smiled, his voice husky as he whispered, "Good, then you're ready for me, sweetheart. We're going to take this ride together."

She didn't even realize that he'd shed his jeans, not until she felt the tip of his erection graze the throbbing warmth between her legs. Instantly, she became aware of the bare muscles of his legs as he settled between hers, the soft silky hair of his thighs tantalizing her sensitive flesh.

Instinctively, she opened herself. Indeed, she was ready for him, *desperate* for him, in fact.

He moved his hands beneath her to cup her buttocks and lift. Then he drove into her, filling her, winding the tense coil within her tighter, until she cried out mindlessly. She grasped his hips, rising to meet him, taking him deeper and deeper, spinning closer to cataclysmic release.

He stared at her throughout every movement, and she found herself drawn into the stormy depths of his eyes, caught in a violent upheaval of emotion as intense as nature's most awesome storm. She even saw streaks of lightning, heard deafening cracks of thunder, until with one lifting thrust they both exploded.

"Together," she breathed moments later, wrapping her arms around his shoulders, needing his strength to quiet the thundering of her heart.

Slowly, the storm calmed and she descended, surrounded by a multitude of brilliant colors—fiery red, soothing blue and of course, warm silvery gray. Peace drifted over, Dylan filled her, and the chaos of her life faded away for a few precious moments.

I—I CAN'T FIND him, boss.'' Mikey's nervous voice carried over Luke Silva's cellular phone. ''I'm sorry. I've been watching Garrett and the woman, hoping Cooper will show up. He hasn't. Neither has Pendleton. It's like they've given up.''

Luke sat in the back of his limousine on his way to a charity walk being held down on the San Antonio Riverwalk. He was a major sponsor so he had to make an appearance.

Appearance was important in his line of work. Not that it was everything. He did his philanthropic part to keep the higher ups in the San Antonio Police Department happy, but he didn't let it get in the way of business.

Nothing interfered with Luke's business.

''What do I do?'' Mikey's voice came over the line.

"Sit tight and keep watching."

"That's it?"

"For now. Maybe Pendleton will show up. I don't think Cooper will just let the woman go." Then again, maybe he was banking on the woman coming to him. Wasn't that why he'd stolen the child? "Sit tight and keep watching."

"Yes, sir."

Sir. That was respect. Luke's rightful due. What Cooper had failed to learn.

But Luke was going to teach him a lesson. Dylan Garrett and Julie Cooper, too.

It was just a matter of time.

CHAPTER TWELVE

HE WAS GOING to make her pay dearly for this.

Sebastian barely resisted the urge to grab the crying baby and shake it into silence. Forget crying. The child was wailing. Screaming.

A full twenty-four hours of near solid screaming. The only time he quieted was while he ate or slept, and even that time was riddled with whimpers and whines.

Sebastian hadn't had a quiet moment since he'd whisked this kid—Thomas—away. He hadn't been able to think or plan. His temples throbbed and his fingers tightened on the handle of the carrier he'd picked up at the first store he'd come to. He couldn't have the child rolling around on the front seat.

At the moment that wasn't such a bad idea. Perhaps Thomas would be scared into quieting down. Lord knew no threats had been enough to accomplish such a feat. He'd talked and reprimanded until he was blue in the face, but

Thomas had only stared up at him through a film of tears and continued to cry.

It surprised him that he felt no outpouring of love for this son of his. But that was Julie's fault, too. How could he have any feelings when the baby was a stranger to him?

Yes, he was going to make Julie pay with nothing less than her life. She'd betrayed him by running off, put him through hell by taking the locket and stolen his chance to know his son.

He had to think—make plans. But how could he with this screaming kid.

"Quiet!" he ordered yet again, but the sound of his voice only seemed to make Thomas cry harder.

"It doesn't matter," he told the child. "You'll shut up soon enough." Once he found solitude. Safety.

And so he'd come here.

Sebastian stared at the ornate front door of the huge mansion cut into the hillside. Luke Silva had done quite nicely for himself.

Up until now.

It wouldn't last. Sebastian fingered the locket stuffed in one of his pockets. The microchip embedded inside the piece of jewelry had enough information on it to incriminate not only J. B. Crowe, but his right-hand man, as well. Silva would soon wind up behind bars with his boss.

Blackmail. That was Sebastian's motive. His trump to get what he wanted. To win the game.

But before he could really start playing, he had to eliminate Julie, and before he could do that, he had to think.

Luke would afford him the chance, or Sebastian would play his trump a little earlier than planned.

He pressed the doorbell and waited.

"TAKE THEM ALL OUT," Luke Silva ordered as he sat behind his desk and stared at invoices for one of his many businesses. He didn't so much as flinch at the command. It wasn't anything out of the ordinary. He'd ordered hits before, though he liked to be the one to actually do the deed.

It wasn't possible in this case. Besides, Julie Cooper wasn't significant enough to warrant a bullet from Luke's Glock. Still, Luke was tired of dealing with the situation. He'd have preferred a nice little "accident," but time was running out. Mikey might lose her again and he didn't want to risk that. It was time to start cleaning up this mess.

Julie Cooper and Dylan Garrett were first on the list.

"Take them out today. I want it nice and clean and quick."

"Yes, sir."

"Call when it's done."

Then Luke would send Mikey searching for Sebastian again. Once Luke learned his whereabouts, he would take care of that weasel for good. Cooper wouldn't get away again.

Never again.

"MR. COOPER IS HERE," Luke Silva's housekeeper announced.

"Sebastian Cooper? *Here?*" Luke was rarely a man caught off guard, but the arrogant bastard had done just that. The man had balls coming to Luke when, for the past few months, Luke had been keeping him under surveillance.

Then again, that was just like Sebastian. Bold to the point of arrogance. He probably figured Luke would be eager to help him, to get in his good graces for when Sebastian was in charge.

Like hell. Luke held the power and it was going to stay that way. If Cooper wanted sanctuary, Luke would give him just that. Permanent sanctuary.

"Show him in.

"Cooper. It's good to see you."

"Yeah," Sebastian said distractedly, as if talking to Luke were a necessary bother.

Luke's chest tightened, but the smile stayed rooted firmly on his face. "So what brings you here?"

"I'm taking care of some business." He indicated the child in his arms. "And I need a little peace and quiet to get everything finished. I need a getaway."

"A hideout," Luke clarified. "Might as well call a spade a spade."

"Very well, a hideout. There's someone out there who knows too much, but this," he held up the child, "is going to bring her right to me."

"That child is liable to bring the authorities right to you."

"Which is why I need to lay low for a little while. The authorities don't know our affiliation. They won't touch me here."

No, Cooper had kept a low profile in all his dealings, Luke had to give him that. Their contacts in the police department hadn't heard Cooper's name come up with J.B.'s or his own. It wasn't likely the cops would look for Cooper at Luke's home.

He rarely let any of his business associates near his house.

But this once he was willing to make an exception. He'd been looking for a way to get Cooper, eager to end the struggle for power once and for all. That's why he'd had Mikey on his tail.

"I need a place to stay," Sebastian said again.

"Of course," Luke replied, his answer seeming to surprise Cooper. Sure, it surprised him. Sebastian knew very well there was no love lost between them. Which made Luke wonder yet again why the man had come to him.

It didn't matter. All that mattered was that Sebastian was playing right into Luke's hands, making himself readily accessible.

Luke stood, walked around his desk and clapped Sebastian on the shoulder. "My home is your home."

"Really?"

"What are friends for?"

"We're not friends."

"We're business acquaintances. J.B. likes you and I follow his orders."

"You are a smart guy."

Luke ignored the comment and smiled wider. "My housekeeper can help with the child." Luke pressed a button and the middle-aged woman who'd announced Sebastian's arrival appeared in the doorway. "Maria, please take this child and see to its needs."

Sebastian quickly unloaded the baby into the woman's outstretched arms and turned away, obviously glad to be rid of the infant.

The man was a cold bastard to disregard his own child. Then again, it was that callousness that had made him an asset. Until now.

"I'll have one of my staff show you to a guest room and get you whatever you need."

"What I need is quiet," Sebastian snapped in a tone that never ceased to rouse Luke's anger. He'd been talked down to as a child, as a poor teenager on the streets, and he'd vowed to leave those days behind. He'd earned respect and power. He'd fought his way up the ladder, and Sebastian wasn't pushing him off.

But this wasn't the right moment—there'd be time enough to put the arrogant bastard in his place.

He watched as the man walked over to a nearby bar and retrieved a bottle of brandy. There was no polite inquiry, "May I have a drink?"

No, Sebastian took what he wanted. He didn't rely on niceties. He didn't show respect.

"Of course," Luke ground out through clenched teeth. "Help yourself to a drink. That's imported for my personal stock."

Sebastian downed a large swallow. "It's good."

"Thank you." He watched Sebastian pace the length of the bar and down his drinks.

"Well," Luke finally said. "I've got a very important meeting. Make yourself at home."

He left Sebastian and headed for the car waiting out front. He debated phoning Mikey and calling off the hit, but then he thought better of it.

Let Mikey go ahead and take the woman out. Garrett, too. Better to have them all out of the way. While Luke doubted Julie Cooper had information that would implicate him, he wasn't one hundred percent sure. She obviously knew about Sebastian and so she was a loose end that needed to be tied up. Garrett, too.

As for Sebastian, he thought he'd found

sanctuary for now. He figured Luke was a loyal
flunky, eager to please. Let him think that, because the more he let his guard down, the
sweeter it would be when Luke showed him
exactly who was in charge.

In the meantime, Luke had a business to tend
to.

SHE HAD TO get out of here.

Julie crawled from between the sheets and
ignored the urge to crawl right back in and
snuggle up next to Dylan. She couldn't. He
made her feel too warm, too safe, too protected.

When she was in his arms, he actually made
her forget the world around her.

He'd touched her so softly, so tenderly, that
for a few moments she'd actually believed in
her heart that he loved her.

Maybe he did.

But was it the sort of love that would last a
lifetime? That's all Julie wanted this time. All
she would settle for. She'd been so certain with
Sebastian, and she'd been so wrong.

This was different. Dylan was different. She
told herself that, but she couldn't quite believe
his love was strong enough to endure what
might lie ahead. Dylan's love could fade just as

Sebastian's had. She couldn't risk that again, particularly since she had Thomas to think of.

Her mind rushed back to the first night at the motel when she'd opened her eyes to see Dylan holding Thomas, smiling at him, *loving* him.

He was so good with her son. If she took a chance on Dylan and let him and Thomas get even closer, a breakup down the road would surely devastate her son. She wouldn't take that chance.

With Sebastian, she'd had only herself to think of.

She had Thomas to consider now, and while she wanted to believe Dylan—to believe *in* him—she just didn't know. The future was too uncertain. Too complicated.

A tear slid down her cheek as she gathered her things in her duffel bag.

"Where are you going?"

"I have to find him."

"We've already been over this. We wait."

"We can do that in San Antonio."

"Sebastian might not go back there."

"Maybe not, but at least I'll feel closer to him." San Antonio had been her home for so long. The home Sebastian had made her flee. "We can wait there."

"Okay." He threw his legs over the side of the bed.

She averted her gaze, not trusting herself to see his dark, tanned body. He was too handsome, and her feelings were too fragile right now. She was so close to believing. Too close.

"Hey." She felt his hand on her arm a moment before she heard his voice. "Look at me."

She shook her head. Not now. Not when she was this close to throwing herself into his arms and surrendering once and for all to the love in her heart. She loved him, but she'd had no proof that it worked both ways. He hadn't said the words.

Sure, he'd told her he felt something for her. Physical desire. But more?

He'd made no declarations. No promises.

"Please look at me." The sudden desperation in his voice compelled her to turn around and she gazed up into eyes so blue and fathomless that she could have easily lost herself in them. If only he would say the words.

"Julie, I—" The words stumbled to a halt as his gaze went past her, to the balcony window.

"What is it? What's wro—"

He grabbed her and jerked her to the floor, his body covering hers. She opened her mouth to scream. Before a sound squeaked out, the glass behind her shattered. A bullet ripped through the air above her head, death closing in on her for the second time in as many days.

And, once again, Dylan Garrett was all that blocked its path.

Dylan muttered a curse and held Julie tighter. Leaning up on one elbow, he dragged them both away from the windows, toward the bed, just as another bullet ripped past them.

Twisting into a sitting position, he leaned back against the edge of the bed and pulled her onto his lap.

Another bullet flew past them and more glass shattered. Fear streaked through Julie, and she wrapped her arms around Dylan's neck and clung to him as if he were a life preserver and she was drowning. He *was* warmth and life, and she needed the affirmation of another human being.

They sat there for several minutes. After the third shot, the gunfire ceased. Seconds ticked by. Maybe minutes. A siren wailed somewhere in the distance. The sound of voices drifted from the street below. Still, Julie held on for dear life. For her life.

"It's okay," Dylan said, his hands at her back, stroking the length of her spine.

With his soft words came the realization that she was crying. Crying, of all the silly, spineless things she could've done.

"I—I'm sorry," she murmured, pulling away from him to wipe at her cheeks. "I'm not used to being shot at...." The words died as she glanced at his shoulder and the dark stain spreading across his coat. "My God, you've been hit!"

"Grazed," he corrected. "It's nothing."

"*Nothing?* We have to get you to a doctor. The hospital. Somebody has to look at it." She tugged at his coat, then his shirt, frantic to get a closer look at the wound.

"Forget it. We have to get out of here. That shooter might decide to move closer and try his luck again." Then he was on his feet, pulling her up beside him with his good arm. "Come on."

"You think he'll try again?" Her gaze darted to the shattered windows.

"We won't be around to find out."

"What about your shoulder? A doctor should look at it."

"We'll head for the emergency room and

call Zach from there. He'll get a team over to the hotel ASAP. Maybe they can find some evidence as to who's behind the shooting.''

"It's Sebastian."

"I'm not so sure. He took Thomas. Why take the baby if he's going to order a hit on you? I think somebody else is in on all of this. Remember that guy I cornered in the bathroom at the restaurant? He works for Luke Silva. I'll bet he's behind this." He grabbed her hand, twining his fingers with hers. "Let's go."

DYLAN STARED through the thick glass of the examination room window to the woman who sat outside in the hallway, a diet soda in one hand.

She looked nervous. Skittish. Ready to bolt at the word *boo*. As aware as Julie was that Sebastian was involved in a dirty business, Dylan didn't think she realized the true extent of the danger they were in.

Dylan knew, and the knowledge felt like a lead weight on his chest because the danger was directed at Julie. His heart and soul. His *woman*.

He'd been about to tell her so, to actually voice what he'd been feeling inside, what he'd shown her with his eyes, his kiss, his touch. But then he'd seen the flash of movement on the neighboring balcony. A sick feeling had churned in his gut and he'd reacted like he always did. Years with the P.D. had taught Dylan caution. He was used to looking over his shoulder and keeping his back to the wall. He'd put too many criminals behind bars for him to let his guard slip.

Especially when he'd worked mob cases with Zach. Organized crime was much more dangerous and more difficult to crack because the people involved were professionals. They were fearless, cautious and deadly.

Sebastian was one of them.

"Now," the doctor announced as he walked into the room and cut off Dylan's train of thought. "Let's have a look at this."

Dylan sucked in a breath as the doctor went to work on the wound. He fixed his gaze on Julie, who'd walked inside the room and now stood off to the side, her gaze following the doctor's movements. She looked scared, nervous, beautiful.

"That should take care of you," the doctor said a good fifteen minutes later. He leaned back and surveyed the white gauze and tape he'd just applied to Dylan's shoulder. "Change the bandages twice a day and keep them very dry. A few weeks and you'll be as good as new."

"Thanks," Dylan said. He went to reach for his shirt and fire streaked down his arm. He sucked another breath between his teeth.

"Easy now. You'll have to use only your right hand for the next couple of days. I'll send the nurse back with two prescriptions. One is an antibiotic and the other is a painkiller. Take one of each every six hours for the next week."

"Will do," Dylan replied as the doctor left the room. Not that Dylan intended to take anything that would impair his senses and keep him from protecting Julie. He would endure the pain and keep his wits.

And keep her safe from Sebastian and whoever else posed a threat.

"He's in San Antonio." Zach's voice drew his attention. Dylan glanced up to see his old boss standing in the hospital doorway. "His car was spotted at The Dominion."

"The Dominion?"

"At Luke Silva's place. The Feds have been tailing Silva for quite a while because of his Crowe connections. They were conducting their usual surveillance when lo and behold, Sebastian's car pulls up. They ran a check like they always do on unrecognizable vehicles, and they discovered he was wanted for kidnapping.'' Zach smiled. ''We've got him.''

''And Thomas? Is he all right? He didn't hurt him, did—''

''Fine,'' Zach assured Julie. ''Thomas is fine and one of the agents on the inside called to say he's in her care. Cooper's not really good with babies.''

''You've got someone on the inside?''

Zach nodded. ''Not full-time. She comes in the morning, keeps the house and leaves in the afternoon. She says she'll do what she can to stay over tonight, but there's no guarantee.''

''We have to get him before then.''

''We will,'' Zach promised. ''As soon as you two are finished here, I've got a car waiting to take you to the airport. You'll be back in San Antonio in a few hours.''

''And then?'' Dylan asked.

''Then we talk to the Feds and come up with a game plan.''

''What about the hit?''

''They picked up a suspicious-looking character in the lobby of the hotel across the street.

Turns out he works for Silva. It seems Silva wants you and Julie dead.''

"But why?'' Julie asked. "It's obvious we want nothing to do with Sebastian or the mob.''

"You know too much. You're both loose ends linked to Sebastian. That's who he's really after.''

"And Sebastian went to his home?''

"I don't think he knows what Luke has in mind,'' Zach replied. "Sebastian may have plans of his own.''

"He's certainly in for a surprise,'' Dylan said grimly. "Silva's not known for being a nice guy.''

"But they're in business together,'' Julie said. "They're both working for J. B. Crowe.''

"They're vying for the same position of power, one Luke isn't going to give up without a fight,'' Zach explained.

"And Thomas is right in the middle of all of this.'' Fear and desperation laced Julie's words and cut straight through Dylan's heart.

"Not for long,'' he told her as he climbed off the examination table. "Not for long.''

CHAPTER THIRTEEN

"MIKEY'S IN JAIL and he's talking."

Luke sat in the back of his limousine and stared across at the man who'd just climbed in for a private meeting. Outside the car, dusk had settled, the daylight fast giving way to night. Across the street, the Riverwalk Hotel blazed with light, the drive full of taxis coming and going.

But inside the car, quiet reigned, disrupted only by the sound of Luke's breathing as he eyed the man across from him, none other than a lieutenant with the San Antonio Police Department, an old colleague and friend Luke had known since the days when he'd been little more than a runner for J.B.'s dad. Things had changed since then. *He* was the one in charge now, and rather than giving him a hard time, Lieutenant Martin Beckham had started looking out for his own interests rather than those of the good citizens of San Antonio.

"He's already spilled his guts to the Feds. There wasn't anything I could do about it. They picked him up in Dallas. A little hard-nosed interrogation and he cried like a baby."

"Who did the interrogation?"

"Zach Logan."

"That makes sense." While Luke hadn't had the pleasure of butting heads with Zach Logan, nearly every one of his Dallas associates had come up against the detective at one time or another. And most of them had done some serious jail time as a result. Logan was good, so Mikey's betrayal came as no surprise.

An inconvenience maybe, but Luke certainly wasn't caught off guard by it.

"Where's Mikey now?"

"In custody in Dallas."

"Can you take care of it, or do I need to call someone over there?"

Lieutenant Beckham shrugged. "I've got a few people on the inside. I'll handle it if you want me to."

"For an extra fee, right?"

"Consider it a special favor." While Beckham had forged an alliance with Luke based on financial need, he'd obviously learned the score when it came to business.

It was all about respect. About playing the game by the rules. Greed had its place, but it didn't override the order of things.

"Do it now," Luke told the man.

"Consider it done, though it's a little late. He gave a signed confession."

"His last one."

"True, but I still wish we had gotten word when they first picked him up. The timing on this sucks."

"What's done is done." Luke hadn't worked his way up the mob hierarchy by worrying over the past. He dealt with the present and made the best of every situation. "We just deal with things as they stand."

"What are you going to do? Thanks to Mikey, a warrant's going through right now for your arrest. I can try to delay it an hour or so, but that's all I can do."

"That's plenty of time. I've got business to take care of at home. The few hours will give me the window I need to tie up some loose ends, then I'll hop a plane. I've been meaning to pay our Brazilian friends a visit. This seems like the ideal time."

"Why not just leave now? There might be a warrant delay, but that doesn't mean the Feds won't get overly anxious and bust in early. They've been known to violate procedure before.''

''They won't if they want this to stick.'' And Luke had no doubt that's what they wanted. He'd been the subject of every federal agent's wet dream for the past six years since he'd taken his place as J.B.'s right hand. While the authorities knew what he was into, they'd never had any proof. They wanted him bad.

He had no doubt they would wait for the warrant, and by that time his business would be completed.

''What is it at home that's so urgent?''

''Sebastian Cooper. We've got a few matters to discuss.''

''Should I be looking for a body tomorrow?''

''You can look,'' Luke said, a grin curling his lips. ''But you won't find one.'' His gaze went to the window. He stared out at the front of the Omni Riverwalk. Inside, the fund-raiser for St. Anne's was in full swing. Luke pulled an envelope from his pocket. ''See that Dr. Milner gets this. Give him my blessing.''

''He'll be very appreciative.''

''Tell him he'll likely get his chance to show just how much.'' Luke had had need of medical attention on more than one occasion from a stray bullet. Of course, that had been in the old days, when he'd had to take the blasted thing out himself.

No more. This was the big time and he made sure to keep a physician on the payroll for just such occasions.

"Logan's in town," Beckham told him. "He's helping the Feds on this."

While it wasn't good news, it wasn't particularly disastrous, either. Luke had long ago stopped fearing the authorities. He stayed above reproach, covering his tracks, playing by the rules like always. And caution was right up there with respect.

"You've got maybe two hours," Beckham told him as he got out of the limo.

"Then I'd better hurry." Luke rolled the window down and told the driver to head home. "It's cleanup time."

"SILVA KNOWS about the warrant."

Dylan glanced up at the young federal agent who'd just walked into the field house where the surveillance headquarters had been set up. The house sat at the apex of The Dominion's golf course, approximately fifty feet from the fence marking Silva's property line. While the field house itself didn't have a good view of Silva's estate—thanks to the massive fence and large trees—the video cameras that had been set up around the perimeter, complete with infrared to cut through the growing darkness, compensated for the location. A wall of TV screens stared back at Dylan, each depicting a different view of Silva's home. There were also audio monitors relaying the information picked up from the various bugs planted throughout the house.

"How do you know?" Zach Logan asked as he left the group of Feds he'd been talking to in the far corner and walked over to the agent who'd made the announcement.

"Mikey's dead," the agent told him. "Apparently, it was an inside job. Silva's got connections. One of our people saw him make a quick exit from the St. Anne's charity thing that's going on downtown. Word has it, he's headed here."

"Exactly where we want him."

Dylan's attention shifted to the headset he'd been wearing. He slipped the device on and listened to Sebastian barking orders over the phone to one of his men.

"I'm taking a few days off, but I want a detailed report of all business transactions faxed daily," he muttered into the phone. "I'll have Hank pick them up each afternoon so I can keep abreast of what's going on." Sebastian had to worry not only about his criminal dealings, but his legitimate ones, as well. The business consulting firm that he headed didn't seem to be getting along too well in his absence.

Dylan took little pleasure in the knowledge. He was too wired. Too damned worried. He'd been watching the house for the past few hours since he'd walked off the plane with Julie and Zach.

His gaze shifted to the woman who sat several feet away in a folding chair, a cup of black coffee in her hands. She looked so lonely and lost as she stared past him at the video monitor he'd been eyeing just a moment ago, her eyes filled with a worry that he couldn't begin to understand.

Her child was inside the house with a murderer.

Dylan's heart flinched at the thought of Sebastian touching Thomas. Then again, maybe he could understand. His feelings for the child, though not his own, ran so deep. Thomas was a part of Julie, one of the best parts, and he loved everything about her.

He barely resisted the urge to walk across the room, pull her into his arms and tell her just that. But this was hardly the time or place.

He wondered yet again if there would ever be a right time and place to pour out his feelings and, when he did, if she would reciprocate. He knew she felt the real thing for him. He'd seen it in her eyes.

But feeling it and acting on it were two different things. She'd made some grave mistakes in her past and he feared her own guilt about that would keep them from their chance at happiness.

Dylan watched as the sleek black limousine pulled up to the security gate. Headlights blazed, flashing once, twice. Slowly, the wrought-iron gate swung open and the car eased past.

"Heads up, people," one of the other agents monitoring the screen announced. "He's here."

"Everybody get ready," the agent in charge said. "Somebody get on the horn and find out the status of that warrant."

"We're still waiting, sir," a voice announced.

"Waiting? It should have been here hours ago. Tell them we can't wait. We need it *now*."

"What's going on?" Dylan asked Zach.

Dylan motioned to the screen where Luke exited the car. He whistled a tune as he walked into the house, two beefy bruisers bringing up the rear. "You think he knows the warrant's been stalled?"

"I'd bet an entire month's pay," Zach snapped. "Damn it. Somebody somewhere needs to speed up."

"Any time now," one of the agents announced. "Linda says she's got the judge's office on the phone right now. They're getting it."

"They should have already got it," the head agent announced. He leaned down toward a speaker and flipped a button that would send his words to every agent in on the surveillance through a tiny earpiece. "This is command. Put everyone on standby. We're nearly a go."

"Come on," Zach said, tapping the counter-top and eyeing the phone where the go-ahead would come through.

"What's going on?" Julie asked Dylan as she walked up to him. "What's everybody doing?" She eyed the group of men who were shrugging out of shirts and strapping on black, bulletproof vests.

"We're getting ready to go in," one of the men closest to them said.

"Go in?"

"It's a bust," Dylan told her.

"Silva is an accessory to kidnapping," Zach piped in, "not to mention an accessory to murder. Up until this point, we've been doing surveillance, trying to gather evidence against him. We've got zilch—until now. The charges will be tough to press considering Silva's got one of the best lawyers in the country, but we can go ahead and pick him up."

"What about Sebastian and Thomas?"

"They're not a part of this operation."

"These are Feds," Dylan told her. "Zach called them in because of Silva's involvement, but kidnapping is strictly under local jurisdiction since Sebastian hasn't crossed state lines with Thomas."

"But he did. He took him from me in Louisiana."

"But you live here and so does he. If you lived in Louisiana and he'd nabbed him and brought him here, it would be a different situation."

"So they're going in after Silva *and* Sebastian?"

"No, the Feds are just interested in Silva," Dylan told her. "The local authorities will follow them in and handle Sebastian once Silva is in custody."

"All we need now is the warrant," Zach said.

Julie still seemed stuck on the word *bust*. "Let me get this straight. They're going to break in there? Just push their way in?"

"Exactly," Zach announced. "It's called a tactical maneuver. The more sudden the bust, the more chaotic it seems, the better. It throws the subject into a sense of panic and he's unable to think clearly. To react fast enough before we nab him."

As much as Julie wanted Thomas back in her arms, Zach's news wasn't the least bit welcome. The armed men around her weren't concerned with her child. They were after their own prey. Luke Silva.

"But what if Silva pulls a gun? What if someone fires?"

"We'll return fire."

"Not with my son in the house. What if he gets caught in the cross fire?"

"He won't," Zach assured her.

"Can you guarantee that?"

"I can guarantee that we'll be fully aware of his whereabouts when they go in. They'll make sure he's in a different room from where the apprehension is made."

"And how can they do such a thing? What if Silva runs right to Thomas?" A vision of Sebastian holding Thomas as a shield in front of him rushed to her mind. "What if Sebastian uses him?"

"The apprehension will be too quick."

"You don't know that for sure. You can't know it for sure. You don't even have anyone on the inside. That housekeeper, the female agent—she left over a half hour ago. I saw her. There's no one inside but Sebastian. And now Silva and his men."

While Julie hadn't been paying attention to the other activity in the house, she'd been watching her son. Praying for him. Willing him to be safe and stay strong. While the housekeeper had been there, she'd felt a small degree of comfort. But now...

Her gaze shot to the screen and she watched as Sebastian ducked his head in and looked at Thomas, who'd started to cry. He barked a vicious "Shut up!" before returning to his phone call.

She shook her head. "This cannot happen."

"We're trained for this exact situation," the agent in charge told her as he walked up. He fastened his vest, attaching the Velcro straps one at a time. "We know what we're doing, ma'am. There's a low casualty rate in this sort of situation."

"A low *casualty* rate?"

"Less than five percent."

"I don't care if it's less than one percent. That's too much!"

"Now calm down, miss, and step aside," the head agent told her. "We've got work to do."

"I won't—" Her words stumbled to a halt as Dylan touched her shoulder, his fingers tightening.

"Calm down," he said, pulling her off to the side.

"I can't. A five percent chance," Julie told him. "That's too much. What if he gets hurt? What if he gets…" Her voice faded as the possibility echoed through her. *Killed.*

As if Dylan read her thoughts, he shook his head. "Put that notion completely out of your mind."

"Why? It's a possibility. You heard them. They have a five percent casualty rate. My baby has a five percent chance of being a casualty." She knew she sounded hysterical, but she couldn't help herself. She'd reached her limit and the tears she'd been holding back spilled over, trailing hot, scalding paths down her cheeks.

"Settle down," Dylan told her again. "Take a deep breath and try to get a grip."

"I've lost my grip. I've lost everything to that man." She pointed to Sebastian. "He's taken everything and I let him. He ripped Thomas out of my arms and I couldn't stop him, and now we're here and Thomas is in danger and—"

"You're getting carried away. Listen to me."

She shook her head. "Don't tell me they're trained for this. I don't care if they've done this time and time again. Five percent is too high. What if Thomas is part of that five percent. What if—"

"I'm going in."

"What?"

"I'm going in first. I'll sneak in, find Thomas and get him out of the way."

"But you can't..." She shook her head.

"Absolutely not. You almost got killed a few hours ago, and you were wounded before that." She touched his bandaged shoulder. "You can't do this. I won't let you. It's too dangerous."

"It *is* dangerous," he murmured, his voice low. People milled about the room, seemingly oblivious to their conversation. Thankfully. "But we don't have any other choice."

"Yes, we do. We can talk to him, try to negotiate. He wants me." The idea stuck in her head and suddenly the answer seemed crystal clear. "We'll trade. Me for Thomas. *Me.* I'm the one he wants, not the baby. We'll trade."

Disbelief flashed across Dylan's face, followed by a deep-seated anger that turned his eyes a cobalt blue. "And have him kill you both? It's not happening."

"I can't stand by and let you risk your life for me *again*. No. Absolutely not. You've done so much already. More than anyone would have done."

"I'm doing this."

She shook her head again. "I won't let you." She swallowed, delivering her final threat. "Zach won't let you and neither will all of these men."

"They won't know."

"Oh, yes they will." She turned on her heel to go in search of the detective, but Dylan was much quicker.

One hand snaked around her arm while the other covered her mouth. He pulled her back flush against his chest and whispered in her ear.

"Think about this, Julie. We're talking about Thomas's life. This isn't a game. Something bad is going to happen tonight. I feel it in my gut and I've yet to be wrong. I don't know what it is, but I won't take the chance that it involves Thomas. I'm getting him out of there. You can try to stop me, but you'll only be hurting your son. Please. Trust me on this. I'll get in and out without anyone being the wiser and he'll be okay. The Feds tapped into Silva's alarm system and powered it off. There's nothing to stop me."

"Except Sebastian."

"Maybe. But if I'm quick enough, he won't know. He's too self-involved to pay that much attention. Please."

She nodded. She'd never been one to trust her own instinct, always fearful of being wrong as she had been in the past. But Dylan was different. While she'd ignored her gut feelings, he'd made a living relying on his, and they'd rarely steered him wrong. When she turned and stared into his eyes, saw the worry and the fear, she knew he was right.

Something bad *was* going to happen, and they had to get Thomas out of there before it did.

"Okay," she breathed.

He smiled then, a slow tilt to his sensuous mouth, and for a fleeting moment, Julie had the distinct feeling that everything *would* be all right.

But she'd been distrusting her own instincts far too long to start now, and so the feeling faded as soon as Dylan turned.

"I'll be back. Just sit tight and keep quiet."

"Wait—" she began, but he'd already disappeared into the crowd of agents clustered inside the small field house.

Within the next few seconds, she caught sight of him on one of the video monitors as he sprinted toward the fence, careful to keep a low profile.

Not that anyone would have noticed. Julie was the only one watching the very last camera. The others had their attention fixed on the monitor depicting Silva and his men as they progressed through the foyer of the massive house.

They bypassed the library, the front sitting room, a large den, moving closer to Sebastian. To Thomas.

With each step, Julie's resolve turned to panic and her stomach lurched. They were too close and Dylan wasn't there. He'd just scaled the wall and started around the back of the house.

Where watching his progress had given her some measure of comfort a few seconds ago, now it filled her with a sense of dread. Dylan was too far away and Silva was too close—

The screens went blank and chaos seemed to erupt as the roomful of agents fixed their attention on the now blank screens.

"What the hell happened?"

"The signals are all scrambled!"

"Somebody cut us off!"

"I don't care who cut us off. Get it back. We need visuals!"

"The audio's gone, too."

"We have no radio contact with the field agents."

A split second later the lightbulb inside the house flickered. The room plunged into darkness.

Julie's heart filled her throat. It wasn't the

blackness that terrified her, but what it meant. Someone had cut their power supply and destroyed central communications. Someone didn't want them to watch, to listen, to know what was about to happen.

Bad.

Dread welled inside her. That someone was Luke Silva, and he was in the house with her baby. And soon, Dylan would be there, too.

The knowledge blared in her head and she found herself shouldered aside as bodies pushed and pulled. A door creaked open somewhere and moonlight spilled inside.

Julie fought her way toward the light and burst outside. Everyone was so preoccupied with the sudden blackout that no one noticed her as she slipped behind a particularly large tree and started to climb the fence.

She wouldn't sit by while things went from bad to worse to...*dead.* The two people she loved most in the world were facing the worst sort of danger. She had to do something.

She had to go after them.

CHAPTER FOURTEEN

IT WAS TOO DARK.

The notion struck Dylan just as he neared the back door of the house—the kitchen, according to the layout the Feds had pinned up in command central. Dylan had expected to see a light shining inside.

He peered into the back window and looked for anything out of the ordinary. Some clue to tell him that someone was waiting. Nothing. The room sat dark, but quiet.

Still, it was *too* dark. Too convenient.

Something wasn't right.

He was this close to bypassing the unlocked kitchen door and trying one of the many windows that spanned the back of the house when he heard the faint crying.

Thomas.

Caution gave way to a rush of urgency unlike anything he'd ever felt before. He needed to be inside. Now.

He drew in a deep breath, gathered his courage and opened the kitchen door. The blackness swallowed him up as he stepped inside.

The crying grew louder as Dylan moved down the hallway, mentally calculating the path he'd planned while sitting in command central with the floor plan of the house. He should come upon the dining room first. Then the library. Then the back stairwell.

Dylan took the steps as quickly and silently as possible. He reached the second-floor landing without incident and started down the hallway. That's when he felt it. His skin prickled. The hair on the back of his neck stood on end. A presence.

Dylan's hand went for the gun in his waistband, but he wasn't fast enough. He felt the cold press of a gun barrel just as his fingers grazed the handle.

"I wouldn't do that if I were you."

Dylan's hand fell away.

"Up in the air."

He complied, raising his arms while the man reached around him and retrieved his piece. The barrel nudged him forward.

"Walk. Nice and slow and quiet." Several steps later and Dylan was ushered inside a large room. A light burned in the far corner and he found himself facing Luke Silva.

"Look what I found, boss. He was creeping down the hallway."

"Probably a Fed." Luke barely glanced up from the task of loading papers into his brief-case. "They more than likely panicked when their power source failed."

"Is that it?" The bruiser in back of Dylan nudged him with the gun barrel. "You a Fed sticking your nose where it don't belong?"

Luke had cut the power supply. That meant the video cameras were down. No one could see him.

Fear rushed through Dylan, along with a burst of adrenaline. His brain searched desper-ately for a way out. He had to get out. He had to get Thomas. No one could see the baby's location. No one could see what danger lurked nearby.

"Packing for a trip?" Dylan asked, grasping for a diversion, anything to buy some time. His only consolation was that Luke Silva couldn't see him and possibly recognize who he was.

"Exactly." Silva stashed another handful of papers into his case. "Take care of him," he said, issuing the death sentence without so much as a blink of his eye. "And bring me Sebastian."

"You heard the man," the bruiser said. He nudged Dylan to turn. "Lights out, buddy." He led him into the hallway and back down the stairs. When they were out of earshot of Silva, Dylan made his move. He jerked around, slamming his hurt shoulder into the man's chest in a sudden move meant to take his breath away.

It succeeded. The man staggered backward, his mouth open, gasping.

Dylan followed him, slamming the fist of his good arm into the guy's nose. The man's head snapped back and his hands went limp. The gun clattered to the floor a heartbeat before the man himself crumpled.

Unconscious.

Snatching up the gun, Dylan turned to head back up the stairs. Instead, he ran smack-dab into the second of Silva's men.

"What the hell—" The man stared past Dylan at his limp partner.

"Don't move." Dylan pressed the gun to the man's temple and instructed him to turn and march back up the stairs, into Luke Silva's office.

"I told you—" Silva began, coming up short

as his head jerked up and he caught sight of Dylan. Instead of panic, Dylan saw a flash of nothing short of pure hatred in the man's gaze.

Luke was everything his reputation said—cold. Ice-cold and deadly.

Not this time, Dylan promised himself as he moved inside the room and shut the door.

"You're dead," Silva said as Dylan nudged the bruiser toward Silva.

"Change of plans." Dylan motioned toward the drawer where Silva still had his left hand. "Pull your hand out real slow and easy."

"Sure thing."

As expected, the man retrieved a very lethal-looking Glock.

Dylan held his gun to the bruiser's temple.

"Come now, you don't really think I'm going to be swayed by a threat to Jack's life, do you? Jack is loyal, but replaceable. They're all replaceable." A shot rang out as Luke fired.

Dylan lunged to the side as a bullet whizzed past. Then another. He heard the bruiser grunt and slam into the floor just as Dylan hit the ground and rolled. Pain splintered his brain and his vision blurred as his shoulder wrenched with the impact.

When he blinked again, he found himself

staring up at Luke Silva, who leaned over him, gun in hand.

"That looked like it hurt." The man smiled. "Then again, think of it as a prelude to what follows."

Dylan willed his shoulder to move, his hand to close around the fallen gun that lay only an inch from his fingertips, but the pain slowed him. He felt the sticky wetness of the bruiser's blood before he managed to touch metal.

His fingers grasped the handle just as Luke Silva cocked his trigger.

THE GUNSHOT cracked open the silence and terror bolted through Julie. She'd meant to simply create a diversion for Dylan. To creep in nice and quiet and assess the situation before giving him the opportunity to rescue Thomas.

But the gunfire changed everything.

Panic burst through her and sent her rushing into the kitchen, down the hall toward the staircase.

Sebastian's voice floated down the hall. "Damn it, he's dead!"

Julie's stomach lurched. With each step, her worry and fear grew. *Dead.* The word echoed through her head, spurring her faster. She topped the stairs in record time and rushed down the hallway.

Then she heard it. The faint sound of crying. It brought her up short, sending a burst of reality through her. Thomas. She had to calm down. To gather her wits. Thomas was alive and he needed her.

Julie drew in a deep breath and slowed her steps. The sound was coming from the end of the hallway. She took one small step, then another. The sound of her own breathing echoed through her head.

"I knew you'd come." Sebastian's voice caught her off guard and she whirled. He cuffed her before shoving her back around and pulling her up against him. "I should have known you were responsible for this. The minute I saw Garrett lying there in that pool of blood, I should have known. Wherever you are, he's never far behind. "

Dylan...*lying there.*

His words sent a rush of dread through her. "He's not—"

"Dead?" Sebastian finished for her. "Thankfully, yes. And pretty soon it will be your turn."

The barrel of a gun pressed to her temple and

her breath caught. But it wasn't until Sebastian turned her around and she saw the look in his eyes, the coldness there, that she realized he was finally ready, even eager to kill her.

Just as he'd killed Dylan?

"I didn't have the pleasure," he said as if reading her thoughts. "He and Luke had it out. Boy," he smiled, "this is certainly turning into my lucky day. When I started out this morning, I had three enemies to contend with. Now I just have one."

Fear gripped her as tightly as Sebastian's cold fingers.

"You can't do this."

"I can do anything I want. Don't you know that by now? *Anything.*"

"Like hell!" The shout came from the shadows a split second before Dylan lunged forward.

What followed seemed a bad dream that gripped her and refused to let go.

Julie found herself pushed backward as the men rolled and tumbled like crazed shadows toward the far end of the darkened hallway. Then a shot cracked open the silence and one of the shadows fell. Her piercing scream echoed through her ears. A sickening wave of fear surged through her.

All hell broke loose as men seemed to come out of the woodwork. FBI agents barrelled through doorways and windows. Flashlights showered the room in light and Julie blinked, desperately trying to focus her gaze. She couldn't see. There were too many people. Too many bright lights.

"Come with us, ma'am."

"Are you all right, ma'am?"

"Let me help you, ma'am."

The voices surrounded her a moment before hands reached for her. She pushed them all aside and fought her way forward. She had to see for herself. She had to know.

A few steps and the crowd parted.

That's when she saw him.

Sebastian lay on the floor. Blood gushed from a hole in his chest. His Adam's apple bobbed as he fought to breathe. But he was breathing. His gaze drilled into hers with hatred and her blood ran cold.

"Stay back, ma'am," a voice told her, pushing her backward. A commotion erupted as a blood-soaked Luke Silva appeared in the doorway, gun in hand. He fired off several shots into

Sebastian's body before a volley of gunfire erupted as the Feds turned their weapons on him.

Luke jerked back into the room, taking bullet after bullet before sinking to the floor, his gun still clasped in his hand.

Julie stared across the hardwood floor at Sebastian. His eyes were empty now. Lifeless.

Dead...

All she could feel was panic. *In a pool of blood.* Sebastian's description of Dylan rushed at her and she feared the worst. What if Dylan was—

"Are you okay?"

"Dylan!" She turned and threw herself into his arms, holding on for dear life. For his life. "You're all right. You're really all right. Ohmigod." She pulled back and just stared at him, noting his blood-soaked clothes. "You were shot. Sebastian said you were *dead.*"

"No, baby. I got off the first shot. I nailed Luke but wasn't sure he was really dead. He went down and I moved to check him, but that's when I heard Sebastian. I stayed on the floor and played dead. With all the blood, Sebastian didn't even question it. He heard your footsteps and he left. I followed him, and then Luke managed to—''

A soft whimpering sounded and Julie looked around to see an FBI agent appear with her son.

''Thomas!'' She took him from the officer and gathered him close, squeezing so tight he squirmed. ''My baby!''

''He's okay.'' Dylan's arm slid around her shoulders. ''Everything's okay.''

''No.'' She shook her head and stared up at him. ''It's not okay. Not yet.''

''What are you talking about?''

''You. Me. We're not okay.'' Dylan had spent the past ten years being a true and loyal friend. But what he'd just done, putting his own life in jeopardy and facing off with a gun-wielding Sebastian to save her, went far beyond a friend's call of duty.

As she stared up into Dylan's eyes, she saw the love shining bright in his gaze, and for the first time, she let herself believe in it. He loved her. He really and truly loved her, and she loved him.

''If you say thank you, I'm liable to go berserk.''

''I love you,'' she blurted, watching his eyes widen in surprise.

"I mean it— What did you say?" His gaze narrowed as if he couldn't quite believe his ears.

But he could. He could believe, and so could she.

"I said I love you. I've always loved you. I just didn't want to see it. I was too scared. Too frightened that what I felt for you wasn't the real thing, like with Sebastian. But you're my true love, Dylan."

"Your last love." He smiled down at her. "Say it again."

"I love you. I love you, I love you, *I love you*." His lips captured hers in a fierce kiss before she pulled away and stared up at him. "And?"

"And what?"

"Don't you have something to say to me?"

"Thank you."

"I didn't save your life and that's not what I'm talking about."

"I know, and thank you anyway."

"For what?"

"For loving me, Julie. You've made my one and only dream come true." He paused a moment and his eyes grew serious. "Almost. You will marry me, won't you?"

"I'd like to see you try to stop me."

"I love you and I love Thomas and I want you both in my life, now and always."

At his declaration, she leaned up and kissed him again, pouring all of her feeling into the one action. When she finally pulled away, she noticed the gleam in his eyes and an answering warmth spread through her.

"Let's get out of here."

"I'm with you. And," she leaned up to whisper in his ear, "I am going to say thank you, and if you fuss, I'll show *you* what berserk really is."

"Is that a threat?"

She winked. "It's a promise."

EPILOGUE

"IT ALL makes sense now." Dylan stood on the riverbank and tossed a stone into the water. The still surface rippled, catching shafts of gleaming sunlight that streamed down through the towering oak trees that lined the bank. It was a beautiful, sunny Saturday afternoon at the Double G Ranch.

A perfect day for an outdoor wedding.

"Sebastian kidnapped Diana Kincaid," Dylan stated to Zach Logan, who stood next to him. The older detective wore a black tuxedo with a bolo tie, black boots and a black felt Stetson like the other three ushers who'd been seating guest after guest several yards away. Rows of white chairs had been set up beneath the canopy of towering trees. Sprays of wildflowers in every imaginable color peppered the area. The slow, sweet whine of an acoustic fiddle filled the air.

Yes, it was a picture-perfect day for an out-door wedding.

Then again, it could have been pouring down rain and Dylan would have still been grinning from ear to ear.

Zach's news that Sebastian Cooper had been Diana Kincaid Taylor's kidnapper several months back only added to his good mood.

Diana, Governor Thomas Kincaid's daughter, had been stolen away right before the birth of her baby and Dylan had been brought in by Zach to help find her. Working as a team with undercover detective Jesse Brock, the men had done just that. But what they'd failed to do was actually uncover the identity of the kidnapper.

"Sebastian did it to prove himself to J. B. Crowe," Zach said. "After that he was basically in—a part of San Antonio's criminal element. It was the one and only time Sebastian really got his hands dirty."

"How did Diana recognize him?" Dylan's gaze shot to the smiling woman who stood near an oak tree draped with swags of wildflowers. Diana, an attractive redhead, said something to Dylan's sister, Lily, and both women laughed.

"The newspaper." Zach popped an antacid into his mouth and chewed. "She spotted all the hoopla about the bust at Silva's house and she recognized a picture of Sebastian. She called Jesse Brock and officially IDed him. Along with that earring of Diana's you found at Sebastian's, it was enough to finally close the case.''

''What's with the antacid?'' Dylan asked as Zach popped another tablet into his mouth.

''Nervous stomach.''

''You're nervous? You're not the one getting married.''

''I'm the best man. It's just as bad. You say I do and your stress is over. I still have the toast to worry about.''

''Who's worried about toast?'' Lily asked as she walked up to them and slid an arm around her brother's waist. She wore a pale-green dress that highlighted her vivid green eyes, and her black hair was pulled up into a loose pile of curls on top of her head. She looked pretty and alive and happy and loved.

''Not toast,'' Zach told her. ''*The* toast, as in what I'm going to say at the reception.'' He popped another Tums. ''I'm not real good in front of civilians.''

''It's nothing to worry about. Just say what a great couple Dylan and Julie make, and then you carry on about how beautiful the wedding is and what a great job I did coordinating everything, and do it all while picturing everyone wearing rookie uniforms.''

"Is this a spin-off of the naked audience thing?''

"Exactly.'' She smiled. "So what were you guys really yapping about?''

"Sebastian's link to Diana,'' Dylan told his sister.

"It's wild, isn't it? I mean, how things have finally come full circle. You helped Zach on that case and he turned around and helped you with Thomas's kidnapping. You brought down Sebastian and he just so happens to be Diana's kidnapper, who the police have been searching for all this time. Not to mention the locket containing the microchip that exposed Crowe and Silva—Crowe won't see the outside of a prison for a very long time.'' She winked at Zach. "I'd say it's bargain shopper's day at Finders Keepers.''

Dylan eyed his sister. "Bargain shopper's day?''

"We helped solve two cases for the price of one, not to mention Crowe and Silva's indictment.''

"We?" Zach eyed her. "I don't seem to recall seeing you at command central while all this was going on."

"What can I say? I'm too busy playing devoted wife and new mommy to bring down my own bad guys. I have to settle for living vicariously through my baby brother."

"*Settle?*" Dylan asked.

"Okay, I'm not settling. I would trade a dozen bad guys for one day with Cole and Elizabeth." She turned and smiled at her husband, who held a baby girl with chubby cheeks and lots of dark-brown ringlets. Dylan's niece. She looked healthy and happy.

Just like her mother.

"You like the domestic thing that much?" Dylan asked his sister, who'd once been so committed to her job as a forensics expert that he'd seriously doubted she would ever marry and find herself a happily ever after. She'd been skeptical, as well, until Cole Bishop had turned her life upside down and shown her the true meaning of love.

Just as Julie had shown Dylan.

"It's heaven," Lily replied, "so long as I don't have to do dishes. Or windows. And Cole trades off getting up at night with me. Speaking

of domesticity—'' she winked at her brother
''—are you ready to get a taste of it yourself?
Reverend Blair is signaling us to start.''

He slid his arm around his sister's shoulder
and squeezed. ''Lead the way.''

''I NOW PRONOUNCE you man and wife.'' The
minute the words were out of Reverend Blair's
mouth, a round of applause erupted.

Julie found herself pulled into Dylan's arms.
He hooked one arm around her waist and drew
her close. She felt the warmth of his breath, the
heat in his eyes, and then his mouth touched
hers. He kissed her wildly. He kissed her sense-
less. He kissed her until she was laughing and
crying at the same time.

''I was going to say kiss the bride,'' the min-
ister announced when the kiss ended. ''But Dylan here obviously couldn't wait.''

''I've been waiting my entire life,'' Dylan
replied as he held Julie in his arms and stared
deeply into naturally blue eyes.

''Me, too.'' Julie blinked back the moisture,
slid her arms around Dylan's neck and planted
a kiss on her husband's waiting lips.

The crowd let loose another round of applause, followed by a piercing shriek. Both Ju-

lie and Dylan turned to see Lily, Julie's matron of honor, standing next to them with Thomas in her arms. His cheeks rosy and his eyes dancing, he smiled at his mommy and gave another shriek—his favorite means of communicating these days.

Julie shared his excitement. This day was the best of her life. As she stared up at her new husband, she had the gut feeling there would be many more to come, and if there was one thing she now trusted, it was her instinct.

It had been telling her all along that Dylan was the man for her. All those nights in college when she'd stayed up late studying with him, when she'd cried to him after a particularly defeating chemistry test, when she'd called him up to talk about her problems. All along, she'd felt the connection with him, the intimacy. She'd simply been afraid to see it for what it was—love.

True, till-death-do-us-part *love*.

"I think he's happy," Dylan said when Thomas shrieked again and waved his chubby arms.

She smiled at her husband. "So is his mother."

"And his father." At Julie's sharp glance,

Dylan added, "His soon-to-be father. If that's all right with you?"

"What are you saying?" She wanted to believe, but she couldn't until she heard him say the words.

"I want to adopt him. To be a real father, emotionally and legally."

While Julie knew Dylan loved her son, she'd never let herself dream that his love would be so strong, so true.

It was, she realized in a crystalline moment. It had been all along, and she and Thomas were alive and well because of it.

She nodded. "Yes, it's all right with me. It's more than all right. It's the most wonderful idea I've heard."

His fingertips cupped her chin. "Then why are you crying?"

She blinked and wiped at a stray tear. "Because I love you. You really are my hero."

"Let's not start with that again."

"I mean it. You're my hero, my lover, my best friend and husband all rolled into one." She shook her head and tried to comprehend her good fortune. Overwhelming to a woman who for so long had never thought beyond tomorrow.

All that had changed now, thanks to Dylan. She had a home here at the Double G, with Lily and Cole and baby Elizabeth and the rest of Dylan's family. She *was* his family now.

"You're my everything," she told him.

"And you're mine."

"Now, now," Lily said as she leaned toward Julie. "What's with all the crying? Your guests are waiting and we've got a party to go to."

"And a life to live. Together. Isn't that right, Mrs. Garrett?"

"I couldn't have said it better myself, Mr. Garrett."

Julie hooked her arm through Dylan's and they started down the aisle, past the rows of guests, who included so many wonderful friends and family, toward the white carriage waiting at the end of the walk to take them back to the ranch house, to their reception and a future that looked as bright as the Texas sun shining overhead.

HARLEQUIN®
Makes any time special ®

If you've enjoyed getting to know
the Garrett family, Harlequin® invites you
to come back and visit the Finders Keepers agency!
Just collect three (3) proofs of purchase from the
back pages of three (3) different Trueblood, Texas
titles and receive a free Trueblood, Texas book
that's not available in retail outlets!

Just complete the order form and send it, along with three (3)
proofs of purchase from three (3) different Trueblood, Texas
titles, to: TRUEBLOOD, TEXAS, P.O. Box 9047, Buffalo, NY
14269-9047 or P.O. Box 613, Fort Erie, Ontario L2A 5X3.

Name: _____

Address: _____ City: _____

State/Prov.: _____ Zip/Postal Code: _____

Account Number: __ __ __ __ __ __ __ __ __

Please specify which title(s) you would like to receive:

☐ 0-373-65090-6   **Hero for Hire** by Jill Shalvis
☐ 0-373-65091-4   **Her Protector** by Liz Ireland
☐ 0-373-65092-2   **Lover Under Cover** by Charlotte Douglas
☐ 0-373-65093-0   **A Family at Last** by Debbi Rawlins

**Remember—for each title selected, you must
send three (3) original proofs of purchase!**

(Please allow 4-6 weeks for delivery. Offer expires October 31, 2002.)
(The below proof of purchase should be cut off the ad)

093 KIT DAFL   **TRUEBLOOD, TEXAS**   **ONE PROOF OF PURCHASE**   TBT-POP   PHTBTPOP

More fabulous reading from
the Queen of Sizzle!

LORI
FOSTER

with

Forever and Always

Back by popular demand are the scintillating stories of
Gabe and Jordan Buckhorn. They're gorgeous, sexy
and single...at least for now!

Available wherever books are sold—September 2002.

And look for Lori's **brand-new** single title,
CASEY in early 2003

Get ready to enjoy small-town charm
with monthly visits to

the town that's the home of the Twin Oaks B&B.
People flock to Cooper's Corner year round to
experience beautiful scenery, warm hospitality...
and some unexpected romantic surprises!

Here's your chance to save $1.00 off the
purchase of HIS BROTHER'S BRIDE
the first Cooper's Corner title.

Save $1.00 off
the purchase of *His Brother's Bride*

**Look for HIS BROTHER'S BRIDE by *USA Today*
bestselling author Tara Taylor Quinn in August 2002.**

Visit us at www.eHarlequin.com
PHCOUPONCAN-CC
© 2001 Harlequin Enterprises Ltd.

HARLEQUIN®
Makes any time special ®

Get ready to enjoy small-town charm
with monthly visits to

COOPER'S  CORNER

the town that's the home of the Twin Oaks B&B.
People flock to Cooper's Corner year round to
experience beautiful scenery, warm hospitality...
and some unexpected romantic surprises!

Here's your chance to save $1.00 off the
purchase of HIS BROTHER'S BRIDE
the first Cooper's Corner title.

Save $1.00 off
the purchase of *His Brother's Bride*

Look for HIS BROTHER'S BRIDE by *USA Today*
bestselling author Tara Taylor Quinn in August 2002.

Coupon valid until September 30, 2002.
Redeemable at participating retail outlets in the U.S. only.
Limit one coupon per purchase.

108227

5 65373 00076 2   (8100)0 10822

Visit us at www.eHarlequin.com
PHCOUPONUS-CC
© 2001 Harlequin Enterprises Ltd.

HARLEQUIN®
Makes any time special ®

Isabella Trueblood made history reuniting people torn
apart by war and an epidemic. Now, generations later,
Lily and Dylan Garrett carry on her work with their agency,
Finders Keepers. Circumstances may have changed,
but the goal remains the same.

If you missed any of the Trueblood, Texas series to date, here's your chance to order your copies today!

65078-7	THE COWBOY WANTS A BABY by Jo Leigh	$4.50 U.S.☐ $5.25 CAN.☐
65079-5	HIS BROTHER'S FIANCÉE by Jasmine Cresswell	$4.50 U.S.☐ $5.25 CAN.☐
65080-9	A FATHER'S VOW by Tina Leonard	$4.50 U.S.☐ $5.25 CAN.☐
65081-7	DADDY WANTED by Kate Hoffmann	$4.50 U.S.☐ $5.25 CAN.☐
65082-5	THE COWBOY'S SECRET SON by Gayle Wilson	$4.50 U.S.☐ $5.25 CAN.☐
65083-3	THE BEST MAN IN TEXAS by Kelsey Roberts	$4.50 U.S.☐ $5.25 CAN.☐
65084-1	HOT ON HIS TRAIL by Karen Hughes	$4.50 U.S.☐ $5.25 CAN.☐
65085-X	THE SHERIFF GETS HIS LADY by Dani Sinclair	$4.50 U.S.☐ $5.25 CAN.☐
65086-8	SURPRISE PACKAGE by Joanna Wayne	$4.50 U.S.☐ $5.25 CAN.☐
65087-6	RODEO DADDY by B.J. Daniels	$4.50 U.S.☐ $5.25 CAN.☐
65088-4	THE RANCHER'S BRIDE by Tara Taylor Quinn	$4.50 U.S.☐ $5.25 CAN.☐

(limited quantities available)

TOTAL AMOUNT	$ _____
POSTAGE & HANDLING	$ _____
($1.00 for one book, 50¢ for each additional)	
APPLICABLE TAXES*	$ _____
TOTAL PAYABLE	$ _____

(check or money order—please do not send cash)

To order, complete this form and send it, along with a check or money order for
the total above, payable to **TRUEBLOOD, TEXAS** to: In the U.S.: 3010 Walden Avenue,
P.O. Box 9077, Buffalo, NY 14269-9077; In Canada: P.O. Box 636, Fort Erie,
Ontario L2A 5X3.

Name: _____

Address: _____ City: _____

State/Prov.: _____ Zip/Postal Code: _____

Account # (if applicable) : _____

*New York residents remit applicable sales taxes.
*Canadian residents remit applicable GST and provincial taxes.

Visit us at www.eHarlequin.com
TBTBACK#12
075 KYY CSAS

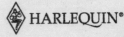
HARLEQUIN®